Spot made a gray-and-white speck in the center of the green vines. Her dainty paws dug among the greenery. Someone would definitely need a bath once I caught her.

Feeling like I'd just played some tackle mud football and the mud won, I finally reached Spot.

"Your daddy would flip if he knew his princess was out playing in the mud."

Then I froze when I saw where Spot had been digging.

Something smooth and slender, about the width of a pencil, protruded from the saturated ground. A bone.

I squatted and brushed some of the mud away. A finger bone, attached to a skeletal hand. I skittered back and fell, cold mud seeping into my shorts.

That bone didn't belong to a bird or a dog or any other animal. I scooped up Spot, getting more mud on her damp fur, and ran for the house.

Other mysteries by Lynette Sowell

A Suspicion of Strawberries

Don't miss out on a single one of our great mysteries. Contact us at the following address for information on our newest releases and club information:

Heartsong Presents—MYSTERIES! Readers' Service
PO Box 721
Uhrichsville, OH 44683
Web site: www.heartsongmysteries.com

Or for faster action, call 1-740-922-7280.

The Wiles of Watermelon

A Scents of Murder Mystery

Lynette Sowell

HEARTSONG
PRESENTS
MYSTERIES

Many thanks to my Cozymysterywriters critique group—Susan Page Davis, Lisa Harris, and Darlene Franklin. I treasure your input, encouragement, and friendship. And thanks to my Centex ACFW group. It's so nice to see other writers in person on a regular basis.

To my family: Thank you for putting up with late dinners, leftovers, and a groggy wife and mom in the morning.

In memory of the original Spot kitty (1995–2007). My feet are colder at night without you.

ISBN 978-1-60260-072-0

Scripture taken from the HOLY BIBLE, NEW INTERNATIONAL VERSION®. NIV®. Copyright © 1973, 1978, 1984 by International Bible Society. Used by permission of Zondervan. All rights reserved.

All of the characters and events in this book are fictitious. Any resemblance to actual persons, living or dead, or to actual events is purely coincidental.

Cover design: Kirk DouPonce, DogEared Design
Cover illustration: Jody Williams

Our mission is to publish and distribute inspirational products offering exceptional value and biblical encouragement to the masses.

Printed in the U.S.A.

*For the love of money is a root of all kinds
of evil. Some people, eager for money,
have wandered from the faith and pierced
themselves with many griefs.*

I TIMOTHY 6:10

Rain pounded the window of our first-floor bedroom. Thunder had woken me at who knows what insane hour in the middle of the night, and all I could do was watch the show until the storm passed. Lightning illuminated the field of watermelons across the driveway. The vines lit up with the flash, and the watermelons among the leaves remained steadfast against the rain. A sudden movement among the vines made me rise up on one elbow in bed. The movement stopped.

Another flash of lightning, and I glimpsed a bulky figure hunched over the vines. So I hadn't been seeing things. Four miles from town, we didn't have neighbors, and our property was flanked by woods on both sides and by the now-swollen Tennessee River to the rear of the property.

"Ben, someone's in our field!" I jumped up and grabbed my robe from its perch on the exercise bike.

"Hold on, sweetie." Ben was on his feet before I could finish sweeping the cobwebs from my mind. "I'll check it out. Though I can't say who'd be plunderin' watermelons this time of night."

He moved down the hallway, and I stayed close behind him. My wedding ring still felt new and shiny on my hand. It and the diamond Ben had given me last July slid round and round as my other hand fumbled with my fingers.

Ben stopped and spun to face me. "Andromeda Hartley, get back in bed."

"No way." I took his hand and squeezed it. "I'm at least goin' to look over your shoulder."

"Those kids better not be out there partyin'. No wonder Mrs. Flanders pulled out her shotgun and chased hooligans off her land. Crazy teenagers."

"In a rainstorm. Right. They'll probably be partying somewhere a lot dryer." I didn't like being woken up in the middle of the night, and Ben's logic escaped me.

He didn't reply but tugged me along with him around the corner then released my hand. A flash of lightning in the kitchen windows made me blink. Ben fumbled with the dead bolt on the kitchen door. Once my eyes readjusted to the darkness, I skidded to a stop on the new tile.

Ben flung open the door and dashed from the back steps, across the covered patio, and into the rain. He paused long enough to grab the baseball bat he'd left on the picnic table after softball practice. I followed. My cheeks stung from the pelting drops, and I fought to see into the grays and blacks of the night. Momma would pitch a fit if she knew I'd run into the rain during a lightning storm. It seems once I got married all my common sense went out the window. Ben and

I stumbled through the muddy driveway. He stopped and I slid into him. He pulled me close and I leaned against his warmth, and we waited until the lightning flashed again.

Not thirty yards or so away from us, a figure splashed down our driveway toward a darkened car that waited at the edge of the drive. Lightning illuminated the yard but did little to help us see the stranger. The car's rear tires roared against the mud, and the car turned, headlights now on, and sped away on the rain-slicked road.

Drenched to the skin, I glanced at Ben. "He sure picked a great time to steal watermelons. Makes no sense. Alone, too."

Under the yard light, Ben shook his head. "Beats me. C'mon, we oughta get back to sleep. Morning comes early. No harm done, anyway. Not worth calling the police over."

"But if it happens again?" I didn't like the idea of someone trespassing on our property. The idea of a silent lurker made me shiver.

We entered the house, arm in arm. I left a stream of water and wet footprints behind me as I got towels from the hallway linen closet. As I backtracked and wiped up the watery mess with an extra towel, I tried to make sense of what we'd seen. I just couldn't dismiss the event quickly, like Ben had. A stranger prowling in the field during a thunderstorm in the middle of the night didn't make sense. Why would someone go to so much trouble to snag watermelons in a storm? And if it was only watermelons, why keep stealing them after Ben and I had moved onto the property?

As Ben and I trudged back to bed, my foggy brain struggled to make sense of what I'd seen. The last thing I remembered before dropping off to sleep was the image of the hunched-over stranger. . .carrying nothing.

"Did you know Honey rides a Harley?" Ben's voice interrupted my dream about us drifting down the Tennessee River on our mattress.

"Huh?" Coffee. I needed coffee, but I wasn't ready to leave the coziness of Ben's arms. A steady downpour pattered on the windows. Days like this, I wanted to close the shades, lock the doors, and stay home, away from the rest of the world.

"She rides a Harley."

I sat up and scrunched my pillows against the headboard. "You woke me up to tell me this?"

"Sorry. I thought you were awake." Ben kissed me on the nose. "Stay right there. I'll bring us coffee in bed. You did set the timer, didn't you?"

"Sure did." I flashed Ben a grin through the predawn light filtering into our room. Most mornings Ben left at five for the restaurant and I slept in.

"Twelve inches of rain in five days, and more on the way." Ben's alarm clock started bleeping, and he slammed it and rolled back to face me. "Mornings like this make me want to stay in bed."

"I know. . ." I gave him a lazy smile and poked one of his dimples.

"Honey's Place is going to be dead this morning." Ben sighed before he gave me a kiss. "The breakfast crowd won't come out in the rain."

"What about the diehards who want their Tuesday senior citizen breakfast discounts? You can't disappoint them." Since I ran my own business, I understood the importance of keeping customers happy.

"This is the heaviest rainfall we've had in over twenty years." Ben sat up and stretched. "We might need a boat to get to town. Should've bought that one I was looking at in Selmer."

"Well, maybe you can. We could go fishing next summer and take our nephews." I moved closer to the middle of the bed. Ben's place was still warm. My kitten, Spot, gave a mew from her place by our feet, stretched, and slithered her lanky self closer to me. I petted her and she head-butted my hand. "Once you get the old dock repaired—"

"The one that's underwater now?"

"It won't stay that way forever." Before we got married, I never realized how Ben was given to sulking. Or at least how often. Now he rummaged through the bureau for some clothes and frowned at a shirt.

"I know." He ruffled the top of his hair, which needed a trim. He'd been too busy to stop by the barber, and when I offered to buy some clippers and give him a buzz cut, he'd balked. "I just don't want to leave you this morning."

The rain rolled down the outside of the window as the dark gray of first dawn lit the sky. "I don't want you to leave, either. But if it's any consolation, I have to go to the store around nine. Someone might use their canoe to go shopping."

"Andi, my darlin', that's a very, very tiny consolation." Ben pulled on a clean white T-shirt and sniffed the air like a hound. "Are you sure you set the coffeemaker last night?"

"I'm sure I did. It should have started brewing at four."

"I'll go check."

"Hey," I called after him, "if you happen to talk to Jerry today, tell him someone's stealing our watermelons again."

"Why don't you give him a call?" Ben's voice floated into our room. "I probably won't have a second to spare once we get the grill fired up at the restaurant."

I wished he was in throwing distance of one of my slippers. The man ate, drank, and slept his job at Honey's. After a mere six months, he'd made himself indispensable to Honey Haggerty.

"Spot-kitty, your daddy's heading out again." She gave my hand a sympathetic lick.

Ben worked as head cook at Honey's Place, the best down-home eatery in Greenburg, Tennessee. The red-haired fireball who ran the place was a good fifteen years older than us, but rumor had it she had a way with the gentlemen, both young and old. Ben, though, was true as the day is long and I had no reason to worry.

We'd been married only a few months, but we'd already settled into a routine. What I didn't like was Ben's twelve-hour days, six days a week. My sweet, hardworking man seemed to have made himself indispensable to Honey Haggerty and her restaurant.

I flopped back onto the pillows and listened to Ben's feet pounding to the kitchen then heard him mutter something about a broken coffeepot. Poor guy. Poor me. We loved our morning coffee. The pot had been a wedding present. Maybe it had a warranty.

I must have ended up dozing off, because when I woke again, the rainfall pattered in whispers and the gray outside had lightened. Spot made a small warm lump curled against the small of my back, and she must have sensed I was awake. She climbed onto my side and started to massage me with her paws.

I frowned. Ben had probably kissed me good-bye when he'd left for Honey's, and I'd missed it. My soaked pajamas and robe lay in a pile on the master bathroom floor. I found a clean pair of shorts and shirt. I'd try to see to the laundry before I left for the store.

Spot romped by my feet as we headed to the kitchen. Ben had brought her home one day a few weeks before. Since I'd never owned a cat and she had a large white blob on her gray fur, I naturally called her Spot. We Clarks had always owned dogs, but I didn't feel quite so guilty leaving the self-sufficient cat by herself during the day while I worked at Tennessee River Soaps.

We entered the kitchen and my favorite view in the world greeted me, damp and gray. The legacy of Doris Flanders' watermelons lived on across the driveway. I smiled. The newest soap scent at Tennessee River Soaps was watermelon, and I had a field full of inspiration. That is, if the rain didn't wash everything away. Greenburg tradition had it that watermelons always grew in this field, and even after Doris Flanders had passed away, someone had seen to it that the field was seeded every spring. And after Ben had bought the property, we'd allowed the tradition to continue.

If Doris Flanders had still been alive, I would have shown her the home we'd built where her century-old farmhouse once stood. But more than likely, remembering the tales about Doris, she'd have come after me with a shotgun, claimed she still owned the place, and tell me in no uncertain terms to keep my mitts off the watermelons.

The broken coffeemaker now sat piled inside the kitchen trash can. I ended up heating some water on the stove and mixing a mug of instant hazelnut cappuccino, a poor substitute but better than nothing. Before the next deluge descended from the heavens, I figured I ought to go across the field and rescue more water-melons. Momma had been itching to teach me how to make pickled watermelon rind, and I was itching to learn. If I didn't bring some melons along to Sunday dinner, she'd let me hear about it.

I slipped on a pair of Ben's work boots and left through the kitchen door, with my feline shadow zipping past me as I went outside. Weren't cats supposed to hate water? But Spot splattered through the puddles in the driveway. Maybe she thought she was a golden retriever or something.

"Spot, come back here!" She barely paused to glance at me then chose to be a cat and kept doing what she wanted anyway.

At the end of the pavement I stopped. Spot didn't mind the wet ground. She zoomed across the red mud of the driveway and into the watermelon field opposite the house. Swells of green melons dotted the sprawling vines.

I clomped after Spot, Ben's boots getting sucked into the muddy driveway. I couldn't bear the idea of Spot getting an urge to race along to the main road and wander in front of a passing truck. My boot caught in a particularly deep tire tread, and I went sprawling forward onto the nearest watermelon vine. *The things parents do for their children.* Another muddy set of clothing was a small price to pay to catch her.

About fifty feet away, Spot made a gray-and-white speck in the center of the green vines. She glanced up at me, and her tiny mouth moved in a silent mew. Then she used her dainty paws to dig amid the greenery. Someone would definitely need a bath once I caught her.

Crazy cat. She had a perfectly adequate, lovingly scooped, *dry* litter box next to the washing machine in the mudroom, and she decided to carry out her business in a flooded, muddy field? I shook my head. The ripe watermelons would have to wait a few minutes.

Feeling like I'd just played some tackle mud football and the mud had won, I finally reached Spot. Now I could hear her mew.

"C'mon, cutie. Your daddy would flip if he knew his princess was out playing in the mud." I leaned over and made a clicking noise. She still hadn't learned to come when I whistled.

Then I froze when I saw where Spot had been digging.

Something smooth and slender, about the width of a pencil, protruded from the muddy saturated ground. Not a stick. A bone.

I squatted and brushed some of the mud away from the bone. Maybe it was part of a bird's skeleton, a rather larger bird. I kept digging and the mud revealed yet another bone. My body skittered back in reflex, and I tumbled onto a pair of watermelons. The cold mud of the field seeped into the back of my shorts. I scrabbled for a handhold and shifted to my knees.

That bone didn't belong to a bird or a dog or any other animal. Its owner had been human. I scooped up Spot, getting more mud on her damp fur, and ran for the house.

Did you hear? The Hartleys found part of a skeleton in their field."

I turned in the booth at Honey's to see who'd spoken. The cushion squeaked. Lunchtime diners filled the restaurant's booths and tables, but because of the varied voices and conversations, I couldn't find the speaker. Word got around fast, and I knew my brother-in-law Jerry would have a cow if he knew people were already talking about my discovery.

After the forensics team had arrived at the house, they had secured the field (as if a pile of bones would threaten to run away). The screaming yellow tape created a perimeter around where Spot had romped and I'd taken a sprawl at finding the skeletal finger bones. I willingly parted with a few watermelons for the sake of investigation. The team gradually unearthed the bones. The victim had lain prone on the ground with arms stretched out over the head. Spot had discovered the right pointer finger.

Jerry let me hang around until I couldn't stand it anymore. I stayed long enough to learn they'd found a set of bones for the right hand, a skull and part of the vertebrae, and a pelvis bone and large leg bones. Plus shreds of polyester fabric. I left when someone muttered something about animals probably digging up part of the remains at one time. My questions followed me all the way to Honey's Place. Ben had to work, and just being in the same room with him and swarms of lunch diners helped me forget the bones a little bit.

I tried not to shudder and took a sip of sweet tea. Where was Di? She said she'd meet me for a late lunch, and I sure needed to talk to her. My sister, my confidante. Ben had given me a sympathetic embrace and a kiss after I arrived at the restaurant, but he moved back to the kitchen where the Tuesday lunch orders cranked out, plate by plate. Honey had fired a cook a few days ago, so Ben had agreed to stay until the supper prep was over.

Part of me wanted Ben to sweep me into his arms and take me outside to his truck. We would go home, and he would tuck me safely in a blanket and make me some tea. Then we'd spend the afternoon in front of the fire. But I knew that couldn't happen. Ben didn't give his word to help someone and then back out. I'd survive.

Someone opened the front door and damp air burst into the restaurant. I turned to see who it was. Di crossed the buzzing dining room, her forehead wrinkled as she slid onto the blue vinyl seat across from me. The jukebox in the corner blared to life.

"Are you okay?" She squeezed my hands. "Your hands are freezing."

I nodded and pulled my hands back across the laminate table. "I've never seen bones from a real skeleton before."

"That one in the science lab at Greenburg High didn't count, did it?"

"Hardly. We used to have fun dressing Dr. Bones. But this? Nothing like Dr. Bones at all. The bones were dark. Not like I thought they'd be. I didn't even realize what it was at first." I watched crime scene investigation shows sometimes on nights Ben worked. Seeing a body on television comes nowhere close to having a front-row view of the real thing dug up in your own field.

"You girls ready to order?" Esther, a fixture at Honey's for years, appeared at our booth. She flipped to a new page in her order pad and touched her carefully set gray hair. I was grateful she didn't ask any prying questions, especially if she'd heard the news.

The soup of the day was tomato, so I skipped that torture and had the chicken-fried steak special. I tried not to think of bones or watermelons. What I really wanted was a few biscuits, topped with chocolate gravy. But the thought of chocolate gravy turned my stomach that morning, and I dared not voice that sacrilege. What self-respecting Southern girl said chocolate gravy made her queasy? At least in my neck of the woods, anyway.

Once Esther disappeared into the kitchen, Di shifted forward on her seat. "Could Jerry tell you anything?"

I shrugged. "They were still digging and taking pictures when I left, but at first look the bones have been there a long time. Jerry said years, but he said he's no forensics expert."

"Was there any, um. . ."

"It was just a bunch of bones, part of the skeleton was missing. They found some clothing fibers, but they probably have to run tests on those, too." I sighed and sipped my tea. "I wonder if they'll be through digging and taking pictures by the time I get home."

"I bet Jerry's in a royal mood."

I nodded. "Ben talked to him earlier. Greenburg PD has had their hands full with wrecks and people getting stranded in their cars because of trying to drive on flooded streets. Jerry about keeled over with relief when the county team arrived at our place and he could leave."

"Poor guy."

"The poor person in our field." My throat caught. "I just keep thinking about who it could be." Someone had put that body in our field. Most people don't kick the bucket while crossing a field and somehow get buried with dirt and watermelon vines.

"You're feeling it, aren't you?"

"I am." A sensation washed over me, of desolation and a broken heart. I closed my eyes, and although the sounds of the restaurant continued around me, the movie projecting in my imagination was of a skeletal hand, reaching up toward me as if in supplication: *Help me.*

"Open your eyes. It looks kind of creepy, and I think the lady at the nearest table wonders if you've got narcolepsy."

I took Di's suggestion and grinned despite the feelings that had rushed over me. A glance around me showed that no one had seemed to notice my imagination run wild. "Sorry. I can't help but think about that person. Who. Why. How. When. Did someone miss them?

Someone had to wonder where they were."

"I'm sure Jerry's going to investigate all of that, or at least he can find out from the county lab. He'll probably fill you in, too."

Our conversation hit a lull when our lunches arrived, but I could only manage to pick at my chicken-fried steak. The comfort food wasn't doing the trick today, but I managed to force a few bites anyway.

". . .Flanders' old field. . ." drifted from another table.

I felt my ears perk up again. Di raised her eyebrows and nodded at two tables over.

"Did you ever go out there during high school?" Di asked.

"To old Mrs. Flanders' field?" I shook my head. "Some friends tried to get me to sneak out there with them one night, but I was getting ready for SATs that summer. I never thought I'd own the field one day."

"I went once the summer after my junior year," Di admitted. "With some of the gang. One of the guys brought a BB gun with him. I learned how to kill watermelons that night."

"You didn't!" Straitlaced Di, running with the wild crowd? Even this summer, Ben and I had collected empty beer cans we'd found among the vines. Kids hadn't changed much since we were in school. I had complained to Jerry once and a squad car had driven by a few nights, but they'd never caught anyone trespassing. Maybe I should have done like Ben and had a casual approach. Even if we'd called the police last night, the person would be long gone by the time the Greenburg PD arrived. And what could I tell them? Someone driving a dark car had parked at the end of our driveway and scoped out our watermelon field?

"That was a long time ago, and don't you dare tell Stevie and Taylor. They still believe their mom's perfect. But Stevie, I think, is starting to get suspicious."

"Ha. I wasn't thinking about telling the boys. I was thinking about telling Momma." I stuck my tongue out at her.

"It's a little too late for her to ground me, though." Di polished off her last french fry, but not before waving it between us. "I'm not like that anymore."

"I know you're not." I took a bite of my chicken. "Um. . .I thought we were counting points for food today. The whole let's-lose-five-pounds-by-Labor-Day challenge."

"I am counting points. I'm also going to work out tonight at Shapers." Di grinned. "So it all evens out. And look at what's on your plate. We've both blown it today."

"I'm going to Shapers after I work at the store this afternoon," I admitted. "I can't go home, and I'm not really in a hurry to, either, especially since Ben won't be there."

"When will they be through at your place?"

"I don't know." I managed to swallow a bite of baked potato. "But I won't go home until Ben's through with his shift here."

"Hey there, girls." Honey sashayed up to the table and placed the check facedown between our two plates. "Y'all managed to swim in for lunch, I see."

"That's right, and lunch is delicious as usual." I noticed tired lines around her green eyes. "Gotta support my man and the best diner in town."

Her gaze darted to glance out the window by our booth. "If this rain don't stop and business don't pick up, I'm going to sell the place and buy me a houseboat and host dinner cruises up and down the Tennessee River."

Di laughed then assumed a serious expression. "Oh, it's not that bad yet. . .is it?"

Honey tilted her head back and let loose with a cackle that made the hair on my arms prickle. "Aren't you the cutest thing? I wasn't serious, I was just playin'!" Several diners glanced in our direction, and a couple of them smiled before turning away.

"Ben said you fired someone?" The question popped out before I could stop myself.

Honey expelled a sigh that would cause the stoniest heart to crumble with sympathy. "I hate having to let people go. But I can't abide stealing. And that Gabe Davis. Serves him right to lose his job. Nobody gets a second chance to burn Honey Haggerty."

"Sorry to hear that happened. I've only got one employee, and she's a real keeper." I studied Honey's expression. Normally she reminded me of a windmill in high gear, but today she shifted from side to side on her feet like a caged tiger.

"Don't be sorry, girl. It's just business. Gabe needed to learn his lesson, and I'm pleased I can be the one to teach him."

"Honey," I ventured, "did you ever hang out at Doris

Flanders' watermelon field when you were younger? I'm trying to find some people who did, or who will admit to being there." If anything big had happened years ago, Honey would be sure to know. Of course, I had no idea how long the bones had been there, either.

"That place?" The shrillness of her voice made the hair on my arms prickle.

"I'm sure you've already heard what I found this morning in the field." The memory of the bony hand clawed its way to the front of my mind. That poor person. They deserved to have their story told.

Honey licked her lips. "Shug, lots of things happened over the years. I don't know. We all got a little crazy sometimes. Throwing watermelons over the Tennessee River bridge, shootin' em with cap guns. Sneaking a beer or two. But I don't remember anybody dyin'." A shout from the kitchen made Honey toss a glance over her shoulder. "Gotta go, y'all. Take care. I'll try not to keep your man too late."

"Thanks. I, um, appreciate that," I said, but not before Honey whirled away, her focus already somewhere else besides our table. Honey's evasiveness looked smooth and natural. She'd probably had a lot of practice. I doubted she was as ignorant about the field as she let on.

"Whew, I'd hate to get on her bad side." Di shuddered. "She always makes me feel like I've ridden a roller coaster just talking to her."

I watched Honey glide to the kitchen area, her head and shoulders visible through the pass-through window by the grill. Her gaze locked with mine once then snapped to a lunch ticket. Then she aimed her wide, toothy grin at Ben.

Not good. But I couldn't tell Di. Maybe I hadn't seen anything. Sure, I trusted Ben. Women like Honey, though, always had a smile for a good-looking man.

The front door of the restaurant swung open and the sounds of rain and storm blew in, along with a man who looked to be in his early twenties. A sound of fresh thunder accented his expression. I jerked a glance past Di. She swung around in the booth as several other diners turned to face the door.

"Honey Haggerty, how can you sleep at night?" Gabe Davis stood on the entryway mat. He planted his feet and reached into the pocket of his olive green hunting jacket.

No one wanted to move. All the news reports swept into my mind, the ones about enraged former employees showing up at their place of business, only to start shooting.

"Now, just calm down, son." An older man at one of the center tables rose from his seat.

"Calm down? Don't you tell me to calm down. You try feedin' a family on less than eight hundred dollars a month." Gabe clomped across the dining room, water streaming behind him. Storm clouds had erupted outside, just as if Gabe had brought his own storm into Honey's.

I couldn't breathe. What if Gabe had a gun?

Ben emerged from the kitchen area. "What's goin' on, Gabe?" *Ben, no!* Maybe someone had already called 911.

"Ask your *lovely* boss, why don't ya?" Gabe stood

eye-to-eye with Ben. "Ask her what she's done." He glared at Honey, who stood by the pass-through window, her arms across her chest.

"You got just what you deserved." Honey ground out the words. "And soon you'll be in jail."

"What for?"

"The cops are on their way, and I told 'em you probably have a gun."

Gabe yanked his hand from his pocket. A woman shrieked. Some diners ducked. I couldn't move. *Ben*.

Gabe held a small white paper bag. He waved it at Ben and Honey. "This is medicine for my baby girl. She's got asthma real bad. I spent my last hundred dollars on her medicine for her breathin' machine. If anything happens to her, I hold you responsible." Gabe clutched the bag and raised it over his head. "No one's going to hire me now, thanks to what you told 'em all. I can't even get a job at Green Lube changing car oil."

A siren wailed outside. Gabe whirled toward the front door but paused. "This is all your fault. I hope you get yours real soon. In fairy tales the witches always do." He pushed the metal bar and the door swung open. He ran off into the rainy parking lot.

My heart pounded, and I realized I'd been clinging to the table edge. Di's face was pale, her eyes filled with tears.

"It wasn't a gun," Di whispered.

"No. We're all okay." I took a gulp of my coffee. Voices murmured around us.

"Ben." I squeezed Di's hand and ran to my husband. "Baby."

He enveloped me in his arms, and he smelled like

bacon and eggs. "Ands, everything's all right. Gabe didn't do anything except make a lot of noise. Just like thunder."

Ben's soothing tones made my pulse slow. "She really fired him for stealing?"

"She said he did." Ben shrugged. "But I have my doubts. He claims she said he could have an advance on his check a couple of weeks ago, and she might have forgotten. We're still tryin' to sort that one out." He glanced over my shoulder, and so I turned.

One of the officers who'd arrived was questioning Honey, whose arms flapped like tree branches in a gale as she described Gabe's entrance.

"And he threatened me, too."

"Not exactly," Ben said and stepped around me toward the officer.

Honey, of course, asked all the diners who would give statements to stay, and they'd get a free piece of pie next time they came in.

I rejoined Di at the booth and reached for the check. "I'm going to write out a statement, but I've really got to get to the store."

Di snatched the check before I could grab it. "I'll take this one today. You've had a hard morning, plus all this happened."

"You don't have to—"

"Humor me. Go. Take care of your store."

"I'll call you later if I hear any more news." My voice rang out like a bell as I stood. Honey was probably rubbing off on me. Several heads turned. I scuttled away into the gray dismal outside, my mood dimming to match the weather. One thing for sure, I knew Gabe would be staying as far away from Honey's Place as he could.

Once I arrived at Tennessee River Soaps, I started coffee brewing and listened to the gurgling pot along with my voicemail. Sadie, my part-time assistant, had called. She was an interior design student home for summer break. Even though she hadn't been free to work the whole summer, she promised to help me run the Tennessee River Soaps booth at Greenburg's Watermelon Fest in two weeks before she returned to Nashville.

I downloaded my Internet orders to the incoming orders file on my computer. Di had insisted I set up a file system of some kind, and now that business had stabilized I was glad for the plan she had helped install on the computer. While Di worked part-time as a bank teller in town, she put some of her business training to use. I, for one, was glad for her efforts.

The bills made a stack of lifeless pieces of paper. Instead of rows of papers I imagined the watermelon field, with bits of brown bone in the mud. The poor person. Alone. Then I remembered Gabe literally storming into the restaurant. Anger and loss.

The phone's ring made me jump. "Tennessee River Soaps." My voice quavered.

"Andi, is that you?"

"Momma." My pulse rate started to go back to normal. "Yeah, it's me."

"You sound real jumpy."

"I'm okay. The store is very quiet today and I

wasn't expecting the phone to ring." I didn't want to get into a discussion about the body in the field. Or what happened at the restaurant. Not now, over the phone with Momma. She'd show up with a pot of soup and want to hear all about it. Although soup sounded delicious, now that my stomach had settled down.

"I was wonderin' if you had any more watermelon rinds for me. Daddy's been hollering for me to get the canning started. He eats the watermelon pickles about as fast as I can make them."

"I've got a big bag in the fridge. I meant to bring them by your house today after I close, but I forgot them at home."

"No matter. You've still got plenty of melons in that field, don't you?"

Yes, and a few bones. And an angry young man who feels hopeless. "Sure do, Momma." I found an empty coffee cup and filled it. "I need to get out there and pick some more, but with the mud and rain, it's been a little tricky."

"Andi, are you sure you're feeling all right? Your voice sounds funny."

"I felt kind of ishy at lunch, plus I didn't sleep well last night."

"Are you pregnant?"

"Momma!" I reached for the coffee cup, and my hand caught on a file folder, which bumped the cup. It slipped from the desk and shattered on the floor. A brown wave sloshed across the linoleum. "No, I'm not."

"I was just askin'. A little granddaughter would be nice. I think Di's run herself ragged with those two darlin' boys of hers."

"Ben and I have Spot. Besides, it's not like I can order up a baby girl."

"I'm not going to call any pet a grandchild. I want the real thing, to hold and spoil and cuddle. And don't get smart with me, young lady."

This was not how I expected the conversation to go. Not talk about babies, those vulnerable blank slates. The thought of having a child around all the time terrified me more than the remains of a corpse in a watermelon field. Most little girls dreamed of carrying a squirming little bundle, feeding it, and singing it songs. I never did. Even when Di came along when I was five, I remember her not being that big of a deal to me. I was more interested in when she'd be old enough to fish with or ride bikes (I'd just gotten rid of my training wheels and wanted someone to ride with).

I taught my church's high school Sunday school class and thoroughly enjoyed teenagers, even when some at church fled at the very thought of them. But the under-twelve crowd? I shivered. My nephews were extremely talented at steamrolling their bewildered aunt.

"You there?"

"Yes, Momma. I was just thinking."

"Well, I'll stop needling you. Call me when you have more rinds to bring over." Momma hung up. I sighed and put the phone back on the receiver.

I'd hurt her feelings, and I hadn't meant to. Normally Momma inspired my confidence, and normally I'd want to tell her about the bones. But I didn't want to talk about it just yet.

I went to find the mop and bucket. The more I tried to ignore what I'd discovered in the field, the more I remembered what I saw. When I crouched down to pick up the shards of coffee mug, I saw shards of bone in the field. I saw Honey's grin at Ben. Now that was something that bothered me more than the bones. The late nights, wondering why Ben had to work so hard. Another thing I didn't want to talk to Momma about. My relationship with Ben was fine, and I didn't want to voice my unfounded worries and bring them to life. And then there was Gabe Davis, reminding me of how precarious life can be. No, he didn't have a gun with him today. But he was a desperate man.

Stop, Andi. I forced myself to do something normal, like filling the mop bucket with hot water and soap. If only every mess were this easily cleaned up, like spilled coffee on a linoleum floor. I trudged to the main salesroom.

Once among the soap displays, I inhaled deeply and smiled. The latest scent? Watermelon, of course. Glycerin soap shaped like slices of the fruit had dark "seeds" studding the bright pink. Melon facial scrub and hand soap were tucked into white wicker baskets with red-and-white-checked cloths to make a perfect summertime gift.

The bones among the vines and plump watermelons wouldn't leave me alone. I knew the county forensics team would be working to identify the body. Was it a relative of old Doris Flanders? Or a vagrant passing through whom no one missed? There was the matter of the stranger prowling in our field in the middle of the night. This morning I'd told Jerry about what we'd seen last night. Someone must have known about the body in the field. No one would venture out in a thunderstorm to steal watermelons. Had they known about or suspected there were remains in the field? The watermelons covered nearly half an acre. Too much to search in the dark. Maybe we'd interrupted them by dashing out of the house. Jerry said we'd have to wait until a report came back from the coroner. He seemed to believe, though, that the body had been there for possibly a decade or more. We'd found a missing person, someone who'd probably been loved and missed, wept over and prayed for.

My thoughts went back to Momma and our conversation. Maybe I should buy one of those home pregnancy tests. Momma had an uncanny way of knowing things sometimes. A baby. Maybe it wasn't just the stress of the morning that had me queasy. After all, I couldn't eat my usual biscuits and chocolate gravy. That surely pointed to something being off.

I trudged back to the office and glanced at the calendar. A red ring glared around today's date—I couldn't forget tonight's Greenburg Chamber of Commerce meeting. I slapped my forehead. Here I'd imagined Ben and me at home tonight, snug and warm inside, sheltered from the chilly rain. He would whip up a batch of his signature recipe Bongo burgers on our indoor grill, and I planned to make a salad. Instead I'd be crammed elbow-to-elbow with the elite of Greenburg. Not that Greenburg really had an elite, but somehow the entrepreneurial mystique made the title of "small business owner" a bit of a status symbol.

Until now I'd felt as if the microscope of the Greenburg business world had been focused on me, to see if Tennessee River Soaps would make it. New businesses always had growing pains. Mine sure had, especially after the horrific time last summer when Charla Thacker died in my store. Murdered, actually. But my business had sprung back and even flourished. Being accepted tonight into the Chamber of Commerce had at last proven to any naysayers that I'd made it.

The phone warbled again, and this time it was Ben. "Baby, I'm hanging in here for dinner. Honey's got a migraine, and she's heading home to rest before the Chamber meeting tonight."

"Okay." I swallowed hard. "Will you be there, too? Tonight is kind of a big night for me. It would mean a lot to have you by my side after all Tennessee River Soaps has gone through."

"I'll be there, but I'll be late. Once the supper rush gets underway the night cook will take over."

I didn't bother asking why the night cook couldn't come in early and take over for Honey while she got over her migraine. Ben's loyalty spoke for itself, and I didn't want to argue with that. "All right. I love you."

"I love you, too. How are you doing after this morning?"

"Okay. Did they ever find Gabe?"

"Not that I know of. Jerry called awhile ago. Gabe's wife said he brought home some medicine this morning and then left, saying he was going out about some job leads. Hasn't come back." Ben sighed. "Not a good situation."

"I don't care if he did steal from Honey. If they need help, I'd like to do something for them. Maybe we can run something out there this week. Something for Gabe's little girl. How old is she?"

"Two, I think. They live in the mobile home park on the south side of town."

"Well, I'll start putting something together for them."

"And how are you after what you found in our field this mornin'?"

A pan clattered in the background.

"I'm okay. It's creepy, thinking about that body in the field, lying there for who knows how long. I almost feel like letting the rest of the field go wild for the rest of the summer. That and I want to find out whoever that was." I bit back any questions about Honey and how she'd seemed to flirt today at lunch. Those questions could wait for another time.

"The authorities will get to the bottom of everything."

"I know, but didn't Doris Flanders have some relatives in town, or someone who might have gone missing years ago?" When Ben had bought her property last year, he'd only dealt with the lawyer and the bank.

"Maybe someone might have some ideas at the meeting tonight. A lot of old-timers will be there."

"What? Did I hear you right? You're not telling me to mind my own business?"

Something clanged, and then came a shout from Honey.

"Baby, I gotta go. Love you." The phone clicked as Ben hung up.

So there I was, left with a phone in my hand and wondering. As best I knew, Doris Flanders had always grown watermelons in the sprawling field next to her home. For once I wished I'd lived out my rebel dreams way back in high school. Then maybe I'd remember some of the kids who hung out there, and if anything bad had happened. Other than stories about old Mrs. Flanders chasing a few partying teenagers off with her shotgun, I couldn't recall a thing.

3

Sweat burned my eyes and I blinked. When I glanced at my reflection in the mirrors covering all four walls of Shapers, Greenburg's ladies-only gym, I had to chuckle at my intense expression. During my workout, I'd been thinking of what I could have said to Ben earlier that afternoon.

"Come home early."

"Honey doesn't pay you enough."

"I wish you'd support me like you do that restaurant."

But none of those statements sounded reasonable once I argued them away. First, I couldn't fault Ben's loyalty to his employer. Now that I had one employee, albeit part-time, I had to admit I appreciated Sadie's loyalty. Also, I knew that money wasn't a big deal to Ben. He wouldn't work at a job that paid him a lot of money and kept him miserable. And I couldn't say that Ben didn't support me. He'd been one of the reasons I persisted last summer when my business's reputation had been threatened.

Now someone's remains had been exhumed in our watermelon patch. I clicked the button on the elliptical machine and gritted my teeth at the increased resistance. My fellow exerciser in hot pink sweats headed for the locker room. Not many had ventured out on this rainy afternoon, but I didn't want to go home so soon. I wondered if the county team had finished their grisly business in the watermelon field.

Ben, I need you. If only today had gone according to my plans. I wanted Ben with me at the meeting tonight, since he deserved part of the credit for Tennessee River Soaps' success.

Lord... I started my silent whiny prayer.

"You'll be at the meeting tonight?" A voice jolted me out of my thoughts. Vivian Delane, nearly ten years my senior and so far winning her battle against gravity, stood next to my machine. She and her husband Curtis had opened this Shapers franchise in Greenburg, and so far the town had embraced the ladies-only gym. After all of Honey's comfort food, we had to work it off somewhere.

"I sure will." I smiled and tried not to glance at the mirror, comparing my squishy lumps here and there to Vivian's sleek frame. Maybe one day, when I was her age, I'd learn her secret. Probably exercising three hours a day. "Will you and Curtis be there, too?"

"Of course." She blinked her cat's eyes at me. Green, with slits for pupils. Contact lenses that had been hip on teenagers. With a clink of bracelets she brushed imaginary lint from her crisp white tank top. "Wouldn't miss it. Shapers is joining the Chamber tonight."

"Y'all were invited to join, too. That's great." I stepped from the elliptical machine. Trying to exercise and talk at the same time was useless and almost depressing with Vivian's form in front of me. In four years I'd hit the big 4-0. If I was in half as good shape as Vivian... Maybe not so bad. I didn't have her catlike litheness, but I had more of a farm girl kind of strength.

Apples and oranges, I told myself. I could probably learn some workout tips from her, though.

She nodded. "I told Curtis if we were going to get anywhere in this town, we'd have to join the Chamber. He balked, but when Roland Thacker told us about the application a few months ago, I filled out the paperwork and sent it in." Her voice rang out in the exercise room, empty except for the two of us. "Sometimes Curtis drags his feet a smidge."

The door behind the reception counter creaked, and Curtis emerged from their office. He smoothed his hair, black peppered with gray. "Viv sort of does what she wants, and I sort of tag along. I heard you had some big news at your place today, Andromeda." Curtis always used my full name, something that made me look twice at his low-key manner. He took his time, not because he was slow, but as if he wanted to give himself plenty of time to sit back and assess his surroundings. The first time I met him, he reminded me of someone. When I told him that, he simply said, "Oh, I get that a lot. Did you ever hear of Brent Balducci?" Evidently he was some actor back in the seventies that made a lot of TV movies, and Curtis looked like the guy did back then, retro haircut and all.

"I'm sure the news about the body will be in the paper, if it's not all over town already." I tried to shrug but it felt more like a shiver. The door of the gym opened, and another exerciser entered and signed in at the counter.

"Whatever happened?" Vivian glanced from her husband to me. "You look ashen."

Ashen. Did I look that bad? I glanced at the mirror. Maybe Vivian was being a tad dramatic. I hugged my waist and told Vivian the whole tale. "And now I'm trying to figure out who that person could be."

"Dear, that's what the authorities will do, I'm sure." Vivian went to her husband's side, her movements sinuous as a cat's. She might be slim, but I'd seen her make the resistance bands groan on one of the machines without even breaking a sweat.

"Viv, you're right." Curtis slid his muscular arm around his wife's waist.

I nodded absently. The Delanes had come to Greenburg about a year ago and opened the gym. Of course they wouldn't be up on the town history, whether it be fact or legend. "The field was a hangout for teenagers. Still is, I guess. Someone was creeping around there last night."

I stopped myself short. They probably didn't need, or want, to hear my story.

Curtis appeared bored then yawned and then sneezed. "Excuse me. I need a tissue. Allergies." He darted back into the office.

Vivian sighed. "If there's a cold flying around anywhere, Curtis will catch it. But he's not going to miss the meeting tonight, that's for sure. And neither will I. Your husband's boss will be trading barbs with Roland Thacker. I've heard at some meetings, they're the floor show."

"What do you mean?"

Vivian moved closer and glanced at the exerciser who'd entered moments before and was now doing crunches in the corner. "You know Honey and Roland once had a thing?"

"Huh?" Not that I really cared to know, but the idea that Vivian had a grasp on a slice of Greenburg I didn't know about surprised me. Sure, we might learn each other's dirty secrets around here, but I learned a long time ago not to "tale-bear," as Momma would put it. Love covers a multitude of sins.

"Oh, yeah. The lady who runs the Victorian Tea Room told me at lunch one time. She and Roland were really somethin'-somethin' years ago. Seems his wife hasn't found out. Either that or she plays dumb. And we're the only ones who know. Well, you, too, now."

Ugh. A wave of nausea rippled through my stomach. "Everyone has secrets, I imagine." Now I had to figure out how to make a graceful exit. Evidently Vivian had done some hobnobbing among the other business owners, as if she were jockeying for a social position in Greenburg, although for the life of me I couldn't understand why. Her husband Curtis, though, acted as more of a silent partner in the business.

"Yes, they sure do. Which is why Honey and Roland hiss like caged cats whenever they're in the same room." Vivian cast a glance at the woman now using the ultra stair-stepper. "Hon, let me help you with that setting." Neat and efficient, she strode across the gym.

I offered a silent prayer of thanks for my chance to escape and went for my gym bag. I determined to make a getaway before Vivian launched into more juicy revelations.

The rain had mercifully slowed to a fine mist, so I took my time crossing the parking lot. I wanted to talk to Jerry about the skeleton, but I needed to visit with Momma. I didn't like the way our earlier conversation had ended.

Twenty minutes later I pulled my Jeep behind Momma's sprawling sedan and tried to avoid the red mud in the driveway as much as possible. The rain came splattering down again, and even my parents' dog, Bark, wouldn't venture out from the security of his doghouse.

Momma opened the back door before my feet had reached the top of the steps. "I was hoping you'd drop by. What's going on?"

"I'm sorry. I just realized I never went home to pick up the watermelon rinds, but I didn't want to go home just yet." I hugged her before following her into the warm kitchen. Something deliciously meaty sizzled in the oven, and my stomach gurgled in response.

"Why didn't you want to go home?"

"We found part of a skeleton in our watermelon patch. Well, Spot did, actually, so I had to call Jerry. . ." I gave a feeble gesture as if that would explain everything.

She clutched her chest with both hands. "A skeleton." Then she frowned as she scanned my face. "Are you all right? That must have been a terrible shock to see."

I nodded, and my stomach growled. "I'm fine. Sorry about earlier. I guess it kind of shook me up a little, the idea that someone had been buried in that field, and no one ever knew it until now."

Momma waved off my apology. "Don't worry about

it. You look like you could use a good supper. Is Ben working tonight?"

"Yes. Honey needed him." I pulled out a kitchen chair and settled at the table. "I can stay for supper, but I've got to leave right after I eat. There's the Chamber of Commerce meeting tonight, and Tennessee River Soaps is joining."

I could see Momma beaming as she bustled back to the stove. "Who'd have thought, a Clark joining that Greenburg group."

"I'm sure it'll be good for business. I finally feel accepted."

"The store, or you?"

"That's not fair, Momma. I meant the business. Not me." I fiddled with the napkin holder on the table. "I've never been into that whole popularity thing. Sometimes it still feels like junior high. Who has the nicest things, the most money, the best clothes. And if you're not in the right crowd, well, you can forget it." I tried not to sigh.

She pointed a spoon at me. "People are people no matter what they own or how much money they have, and don't you forget it. Money can poison the best of relationships. Havin' it, or needin' it." Her eyes looked shadowed for a moment, but she turned back around to the stove.

"I wonder who was buried in our field," I blurted.

"Kids went out there a lot, I know. Even before you were born. Even your sister went there as a teenager."

I tried not to gape. "You knew about that?"

Momma nodded. "I saw the dry mud on her shoes

early Sunday mornings and heard her sneaking in through the back door once. She didn't know I knew. I got calluses on my knees over that girl. Right after that she straightened out when she broke up with one particular guy. I'm glad the Lord knocked some sense into her, because her daddy and I sure couldn't. Short of putting bars on her bedroom window, I didn't know what to do."

Now it was my turn to nod. "The guy Diana dated her senior year."

"Seems datin' the wrong guy runs in the family. Jewel would never listen to our momma and daddy. I'm just glad both you and your sister found the right men." Momma shook her head. "I never wanted either one of you to turn out like your aunt Jewel."

At the mention of my aunt's name, I had a memory of laughter and golden hair and blue eyes, with a smile like summer. I was five, and Aunt Jewel had taken me fishing on the river, its reflected light making her glow like an angel. Then she was gone, and my mind shuffled to a series of family memories. She left Greenburg without telling anyone good-bye when she turned eighteen and never looked back. The betrayal still echoed through our family, years later.

"I'm glad the Lord gave me Ben." I swallowed hard and brushed the memory aside. "It took me forever to quit being stupid, but I'm glad he waited for me."

"You and Diana are both blessed. There's just one more thing I'd like. Not a thing, really, though."

"What's that?" I knew what was coming and braced myself.

"A little granddaughter." Momma raised her hand.

"I know. You didn't let me say my piece earlier."

"Ben and I have only been married for a few months. I'm hardly used to being married yet, let alone thinking about becoming a mother."

"I know. But in a few years you'll be forty, and year after year the chances of you"—here Momma blushed—"conceiving. . .get smaller and smaller."

"I know," I said. "We'll start a family. I promise. It's just so fast."

"Honey, life comes fast. Just ask your daddy. He's retirin' for good at the end of the year."

"Retiring?" I breathed easier at the change in subject. Of course, Momma could swing the conversation back around to babies. "Is he feeling okay?"

"He's fine. He just decided he wanted to take things easier. We're talkin' about doing some traveling. He wants to get a travel trailer to pull behind the truck. We might go up to Branson and catch some shows. I've always wanted to see the Grand Canyon. Or Florida sounds nice."

"That's great." I could picture them arguing about which exit to take on some freeway, or better yet, cruising along some forgotten highway on an adventure. Daddy always seemed to be more the adventurer, and Momma was always happiest at Daddy's side.

"This is why I'm telling you to start that family as soon as you can. Don't say you can't afford it, or you don't have the time, or it's too much of a hassle." She blinked as she turned to the sink to wash her hands.

"What's wrong? What aren't you telling me? Are you or Daddy sick?" My throat caught at the very idea.

"No, we're fine except for aches and pains and your daddy's general crankiness." Momma poured herself a fresh cup of coffee and joined me at the table. "It's your Papaw. He's not doing good. I think his Alzheimer's is getting worse."

"Oh, Momma." I touched her hand. "I know I should go see him."

"That's why I'm saying. You just can't put things off forever."

"Papaw. . .he always told the funniest jokes and hid candy in his pockets." Now my own vision blurred. Time had crept along, and while I'd taken my sweet time building my own life, Papaw had waited to the side. I knew he'd stayed in the same room for nearly ten years now, surrounded by family pictures and some of Grandma's crocheted pillows. He clung to what memories he still owned.

"I still feel bad about putting him in a nursing home. But he's strong even if his mind isn't, and your daddy didn't think we could keep him here. He'd hurt himself or break something or run off. If Jewel were around, I know we'd have figured something out together."

"I should go see him."

"He asks about you and your sister every time I visit."

"I wouldn't know what to say. What if he's confused, and I make him mad?"

"Just talk. He'll do all right, and you can usually tell when he drifts off. Don't take it to heart if he hollers at ya, though." Momma shook her head. "I sometimes wonder if his troubles started after Jewel left. It broke his heart. I tried to make him happy, bringin' you girls around to the house...but then when he lost Momma... it was like his brain gave up trying to make sense of everyday things most people don't forget."

The sound of sizzling meat grew louder, and my stomach growled.

"I'd better check on that roast."

I shivered. "I'm glad we've all got each other."

"I'm glad of that, too."

"But the body in the field. The idea makes me so sad, to think of someone's daughter or son, or sister or brother lying there. Didn't anyone miss them or wonder where they were?" My mind spun with possibilities. "I need to find something out if I can. You know how the authorities can move so slowly."

"Jerry's a good man. Maybe not the speediest officer in the bunch, but he does his best to do right by the law, I'm sure."

"I don't mean Jerry. I mean the county coroner."

The phone's ring made Momma and me both give a start. She went to answer it, and I decided to wash the few dishes in the sink. I couldn't stay still for long, not when my thoughts ran rampant with questions I wanted to ask. I'd try to dig up any news of any parties gone bad out at the watermelon patch.

Momma came back to the table. "Well, that was an interesting phone call."

"What's goin' on?" At the look on Momma's face, I wanted to pray right then and there.

"Those slow authorities aren't letting the grass

grow under their feet. It was Jerry, putting a bug in my ear that I should probably release Jewel's dental records to the county."

"Why?"

"It seems the remains in your field belonged to a woman, and it seems when Jewel left without a word, your Papaw filed a missing persons report."

4

Roland Thacker leaned against the podium and glared at Honey Haggerty. "Miss Haggerty. . ." His *sssss* in Miss almost sounded like a snake. "Are you quite finished?"

"I don't know. Can't really say." Honey flipped a bouncy red wave over her shoulder and gave a toss of her head. "Guess I'm finished for tonight." As she sat down, she glared at Roland then winked at him. She shot me a grin.

The Greenburg City Hall auditorium sounded large, but it really only had a capacity of about fifty. We had thirty in the room and I could hardly breathe. Someone's antiperspirant had given out an hour ago. We were still hashing out the details of each committee for the annual Watermelon Festival. After every committee report, someone expressed a complaint about how the committee had executed their plans, which led to someone on the committee getting upset and threatening to quit. Junior high school was right. Did I really want to join a group like this? I saw Trudy from the coffee shop. She smiled and waved. Nothing seemed to ruffle her. Tonight her long hair hung in two braids down the back of her seat.

Vivian Delane's earlier remarks about an affair between Honey and Roland whispered in my ears. I wanted to cleanse my mind, but even now I couldn't ignore the fact that these two had some kind of history.

His aggravation with her was understandable, because Honey was the kind of person most people had strong sentiments about, one way or another.

Lightning flashed outside. The approaching storm gave Roland a great cover for getting Honey to be quiet. No one wanted to be stuck driving home during a downpour at night.

The seat next to me had remained empty throughout the meeting. Where was Ben? I'd already been called up to the platform at the front of the room, along with Vivian and Curtis, as the newest business members of the Chamber. Somehow during the course of the night, I'd landed a position on the Watermelon Festival vendor clearance committee. Another member had to step down, so I ended up taking her spot. It probably had something to do with Honey's steamrolling. I didn't know whether to thank her or pray for strength.

A burst of wind from the hall outside made the curtains swirl. Here came Ben, the little lines around his eyes more prominent after his twelve-hour day. And his smile was just for me. He slid onto the empty chair next to mine.

I tried not to wrinkle my nose at his smell. But then his sweet kiss on my cheek made me forget the aroma of the grill. "I'm glad you made it."

Ben slid his arm around me. "Got here as fast as I could." My earlier aggravation about him working late evaporated. "Did I miss anything?"

The sound of a gavel echoed against the paneled walls. "Meeting adjourned." Chairs squeaked as bodies shifted to stand. My back complained when I stood.

"I'm not sure. Some parts I might have zoned out."

Call it fatigue catching up with me after a stressful day or call it boredom, but I think it was really pre-occupation. The skeleton's identity had followed me through the rainslicked streets of Greenburg and taken up space in Ben's empty chair. I knew what my gut told me, especially after hearing Momma's voice earlier that afternoon telling me about the dental records and the missing persons report. She still couldn't believe Papaw had never told them about filing the report. Maybe it was a matter of pride that he couldn't have believed Jewel would willingly leave us. But the things people do for love sometimes. . .

That body had to be my aunt Jewel, and someone had put her there. Then they sat back and let the rumors fly, that she had run off with somebody and broken her family's heart. Maybe I was making an assumption, maybe not, but knowing someone's loved one had lain in that field for years, I couldn't let it rest.

"You okay? You look a little tired." Ben rubbed my back.

"It's been a long day. But I need to talk to someone before we leave." I eyed the crowd. Who to talk to first? Long-timers around my aunt's age. . .had she lived. Roland Thacker I'd leave be for now. One of his daughters had been killed in my store, and because of my sleuthing, his other daughter was serving time for her murder. I still had a hard time looking him in the eye. It was hard to imagine the pain he and his wife had gone through. I'd been told once, "You're not a parent. You wouldn't understand." But I still felt like Roland held me responsible for losing both of his daughters.

Honey Haggerty divided the meeting room as if it were the Red Sea. She headed for the doors, heads turning in her wake. Well, she was a little older than Aunt Jewel would have been now, but Honey probably knew something about her. I'd talk to her again tomorrow. I knew right where she'd be, and if she tried to fool me by being vague like she had earlier today, I'd show her I could equal her in the stubborn department.

"Who are you looking for?"

"Someone who might have known my aunt Jewel." There went Greta Maynard, who owned a quilt shop and a bed-and-breakfast in her family's antebellum mansion on the river. I had a hard time picturing any of the fifty-and-over crowd sneaking out to party in a watermelon patch.

Ben grabbed my arm and stopped my movement. "Hang on, now. What's this about?" But his touch softened.

"I think that body in the field is my aunt Jewel. No, the reports aren't back. All I know is what Jerry told Momma. At first look, what they found likely belongs to a Caucasian female in her late teens, early twenties. And Momma said my grandfather filed a missing persons report after Aunt Jewel disappeared." I watched Greta vanish through the doors. Here I was losing my chances to start getting some answers because everyone was scurrying for home like rats leaving a sinking ship.

"That's only a guess on your part."

I slung my bag over my shoulder. "Maybe so, but Aunt Jewel would have called us or something. Even if she left town."

"I'm tired. Let's go home." Ben's dimple winked at me. Okay. We'd been apart forever, it seemed, and here I was dragging my heels to go home. A haunted look from Roland Thacker spurred me out the door at last. His daughter Melinda would likely be released from prison in a few years. Plea bargain added to good behavior and parole.

The warmth of Ben's hand comforted me as we walked into the night. Voices echoed across the parking lot. Honey and Junker Joe Toms, hollering in their classic fashion under the glare of the parking lot lights. An occasional lightning flash accentuated their conversation. They must have noticed us, because Honey's volume dropped to a normal speaking level.

"My mind's made up, and ain't you or no one else gonna change it." She waved at us, then flashed a smile before transforming it into a glare at Joe. "Besides, what's done's done."

"How do you do it?" I whispered to Ben as he unlocked his truck. "I'd spend every workday taping my mouth shut so I wouldn't say something that would get me fired."

"Honey has no bite. Lots of bark, though. And I can ignore barking."

A gravelly voice drifted towards us. "Someone's gonna knock you upside that hard head o' yours one day, and when they do, don't come cryin' to me." Junker Joe stomped to his rattletrap motorbike, then kick-started it as if Honey were under his foot.

"Aw, go on with you then!" Honey shook her head.

I shook mine, too, before giving Ben a kiss. "I'll

meet you at the house."

"We'll get a fire lit." He gave me another long, slow kiss. *I just love being married. . . .*

Another crack of lightning gave extra light to my path as I headed to my Jeep. Here came the first raindrops. From the corner of my eye, I saw Honey heading toward Ben's truck. His engine roared, headlights came on.

"Oh, Ben, Ben," came Honey's singsong voice. "Can I ask you somethin' real quick?"

I suppose I could have waited, but Ben started backing up his truck, so I figured he would follow. A check in the rearview mirror as I drove along Main Street revealed no truck. I bit my lip. Sure, I trusted Ben, but I didn't appreciate more precious time being stolen from us.

Thirty minutes later I had a fire roaring in our fireplace and coffee brewing in the pot. Still no Ben. I punched his cell phone number. Spot lurked at the edge of the hallway. Her look told me it was too late for anyone to be out.

"Ben, are you almost home?" I asked when he answered.

"I'm on my way. I had to circle around. The other road was closed because of the rain. I had to jumpstart Honey's vehicle. The battery was dead."

"I'll be waiting for you."

"I'm hurrying."

"Just be careful."

Twenty minutes later I saw the flicker of headlights as Ben's truck bumped along the muddy driveway.

Finally. My cup of coffee was cold, and I tried not to yawn. So much for a romantic refuge tonight. Well, at least we'd be safe and cozy.

"I'm home," Ben called from the kitchen, the sound of wind and rain entering with him.

"The coffee's still on. Mine needs warming, though." We met in the kitchen, and Ben took me in his arms.

"Ew, you're soaked. That's been happening a lot lately." But I kissed him anyway. "Get some coffee and meet me in the living room. Are you hungry? I can reheat something."

"Nah, I don't want the heartburn to kick in." Ben took a mug from the cabinet and poured himself a cup of coffee.

We settled on the love seat near the fireplace. As I watched the dancing flames, Aunt Jewel came back to mind. I had to ask Momma the bunches of questions I'd never asked, such as what would have made her leave without a word. Worse, who'd put her in that field.

I started telling Ben about Jerry's phone call earlier. "Momma got pretty upset, but she wouldn't talk about Aunt Jewel's disappearance. Then when Daddy got home, I expected Momma to talk to him, but she didn't."

"I'm sure she'll say something when she's ready." Ben's arm around me tightened.

"I hope so. If that skeleton turns out to be Aunt Jewel, Momma's really going to need us. And she's always the strong one. But if she needs us. . ."

"I know you and your daddy and Diana will be there for her."

We fell silent and watched the flames lick up the wood. Funny, using the fireplace in August, but the latest storm had arrived with a cool front.

"Oh, I meant to tell you. Honey wants to talk to us tomorrow morning, after the breakfast rush is over." The reflected firelight danced off Ben's tired eyes.

"Good, I need to talk to Honey about Aunt Jewel. According to what little information Momma gave me, Honey and Aunt Jewel used to be friends years ago." My heart skittered a bit. "Did she say what she wanted to talk to us about?"

"It involves my job at the restaurant, and that was all she said."

"Was she hollering at you when she asked?"

"No, she grinned at me like I was her long-lost nephew. Or something."

Or something was right. Honey didn't seem to be the type of woman to have nephews, long-lost or otherwise. She sure had a grin for a good-looking man, no matter what his age. Junker Joe had stuck with her for years, and I couldn't imagine why. If Ben was as "friendly" with women as Honey was with men, I'd be keeping him on a tight leash. But then I trusted him and didn't need to. His kind of friendly had nothing to do with flirting. Nice guys like Ben, though, seemed to attract women who thrived on male attention. I frowned.

"I guess we'll have to wait and see then. It'll be the perfect chance for me to talk to her about Aunt Jewel."

"Still got that idea in your head?"

"Yup. And I'm not about to let go of my suspicion until I get a good answer from someone. Or a confirmation or denial from the authorities."

"Not to change the subject, but did you mention something about being on a Watermelon Festival committee?"

"Yes, I am. Honey actually had a lot to do with that, too. I'm on the vendor committee, helping make phone calls. The Chamber wants all the businesses to stick close to the watermelon theme, so they have a vendor committee. This is going to be an old-fashioned country fair, and we don't want a lot of 'plastic inflatable junk and bangles,' as Honey put it. I agree with her about that point. A country fair shouldn't peddle plastic stuff that you can buy anywhere. We need to make this fair distinctly Greenburg."

"I'm proud of you." Ben sounded like his voice caught. He stared at the fire instead of looking me in the eye.

"Thanks. And I owe my success to you. I wanted to quit the business last year. But you wouldn't let me."

"You're right." This time he looked at me and smiled, but his eyes remained somber. "Did you take notes at the meeting tonight?"

"That I did. I'll go grab them." Along with the suspect list I'd left in the kitchen. By the time I got back to the living room, Ben's eyes were closed, his mouth open, and his breathing slow. I planted a kiss on his forehead. "I love you, tired man."

I couldn't reach the ringing phone. The blankets wouldn't cooperate and let me move, but finally my hand found the plastic receiver. The clock read five. Ben had already gone to work, and I hadn't even heard him leave.

"Hello?" I wondered who was calling this time of morning. Phone calls too early or too late never meant good news. Maybe someone had simply dialed the wrong number. Then the only bad news would be a few minutes of lost sleep for me.

"I hate to wake you, Andi, but. . ." Ben sounded infinitely tired.

"Where are you? What's wrong?" I shoved the blankets aside and sat upright in bed.

"I'm at the restaurant, waiting for the police to arrive."

My mind was slow and sluggish. "Was there a break-in?"

"No, babe. It's Honey. She's dead."

5

I threw on some respectable clothes and dashed into the drizzle. Ben needed me. He didn't say so, but as I zoomed along the wet roads, I prayed. The Lord knew I'd been complaining more than praying lately. Easy enough and natural enough to slip into. But praying was a better use of my breath. Honey. Dead. I blinked back tears. The crusty redhead hadn't always made it easy for me to act like a Christian, and I'd readily admitted to myself she inspired a jealous streak in me, but dead?

Of course, Jerry, chief of police and Ben's brother, would be on his way. Unless protocol or conflict-of-interest or something meant he couldn't because of Ben. I wasn't sure about those kinds of details, but Jerry was a pretty by-the-book guy. And maybe Honey had died of natural causes. Yet Honey had always seemed quite active and healthy.

Red-and-blue lights flashed off the exterior of Honey's Place and competed with her light-up sign by the road proclaiming the best pies in Greenburg lived here. . .but not for long. Not without Honey to make her signature pies. Some people forgave Honey her faults because of her baking, but evidently someone hadn't. A lone squad car sat in the parking lot next to Ben's truck and Honey's motorcycle.

Ben waited by the glass double doors to the restaurant, his face registering surprise when he saw my Jeep. I joined him under the awning where diners could pull up in the rain and drop off passengers. I gave him a wordless hug then stood back and searched his face for answers

He gestured with his head in the direction of the dining room just inside the doors. "I found her back in the kitchen. Jerry's waiting for the county crime team to arrive."

"What happened?" I watched as Jerry approached the doors from inside and joined us under the awning. Now lights blazed inside the restaurant.

"She choked on watermelon rind. I found her by the chopping block. She was working on her newest recipe, watermelon-rhubarb pie."

"Those details aren't for public knowledge." Jerry peeled off some gloves. "You know you can't say anything to anyone. I believe we're looking at a homicide here. If she'd choked on one bite of watermelon, she wouldn't have ended up with rind in her throat and filling her mouth."

I shuddered at the picture he painted, then took a deep breath. "We won't say anything," I promised him. "Any sign of forced entry?"

Jerry shook his head. "Not from what Ben says."

"Like I said, I was getting here at five to light the grill and get ready for breakfast." Ben blinked hard and then wiped his eyes.

"She'd been here awhile." Jerry shook his head. "The forensics team will learn more, but I'd guess she was there most of the night."

Ben glanced at me. "She must have come back to the

restaurant after the Chamber of Commerce meeting."

Jerry glanced at Ben with narrowed eyes. "So you saw her last night?"

"After the meeting, her battery was dead on her car," Ben said. "I helped her jump-start her car before I left. She must have picked up her Harley at home and headed to the restaurant later."

My spine prickled.

Jerry frowned. "You can stop right there."

I already guessed what he was getting at. I turned to Ben. "Honey, you were probably the last one to see Honey before someone killed her."

Ben drew me into his arms. "I don't think we'll open the restaurant today."

I looked over at Jerry. "Should Ben get a lawyer?"

Jerry's round and normally kind face looked grim in the lights. "Andi, it's too early to say right now. Honey had equal amounts of friends and enemies here in town."

"We're going to hire a lawyer," I said. "Steve can ask his cousin who'd be good." I knew that Di's husband having relatives in high places would come in handy someday. Ben's arms didn't hold the comfort for me they usually did, as if he'd gone numb and they'd frozen in place.

Headlights flickered in the parking lot, and I didn't have to squint to know it was the coroner's van arriving along with the team. And here I was again with a front-row view for the second time in as many days.

"I should call the staff." Ben released me and reached for his cell phone on his belt. He called Esther first. I could hear her gasp and start to cry. My heart went out to the older woman. She needed her job, needed those tips and customers to help supplement her fixed income.

"Jer—" He'd started toward the coroner's van but paused when I called him. I figured I'd ask Jerry a few questions while Ben was on the phone.

"What's that?"

"Who could have done this? I know you said Honey wasn't exactly popular with some people. . ." My first thought drifted to Gabe Davis. But he wasn't the only person whose anger Honey managed to ignite with her flintlike personality.

"We're going to find out."

Another name jolted my caffeine-deprived brain. "Junker Joe. He and Honey were fighting last night after the Chamber of Commerce meeting."

"Physically?" Jerry's brow furrowed.

"No, as in yelling at each other. I know their fights are probably legendary, but this one *was* last night."

"You don't have to tell me legendary. I've gotten calls from some neighbors hearing shouting and occasionally glass breaking, either at his place or hers. So what was this fight about?"

"I don't know exactly. All I can remember is her saying something about him not being able to change her mind."

"Okay. I'll be questioning Joe, anyway. I'll see what that turns up." Doors slammed on the coroner's van, and both Jerry and I looked as the team removed their gear.

"I know you're going to investigate Ben. You have

to. And he came home late last night. He was one of the last people to see her alive. But he wouldn't have done this." I definitely didn't like the direction my thoughts headed.

"You think I don't know my brother? Of course I don't think he did it." Jerry faced me again and planted one hand on his hip. "I've got to give the DA all the information I have, including Ben's whereabouts last night. Not happy about it, but I've got to."

"I'm not asking you to withhold information. I just want every stone turned, every lead followed. I don't care how silly or far-fetched." My face flushed. I'd had experience with what sounded silly and far-fetched last year, but I'd been right and found a murderer. Which reminded me of Vivian's intimations about Roland Thacker.

"You sound like the DA." His smile looked forced. He glanced back toward the team that approached, carrying their gear. "Let me show you what we've got here, Stu. Sorry about the early hour."

The team leader resembled a bulldog. He shook Jerry's hand with one of his stubby ones. "Don't apologize. Corpses don't keep normal business hours."

I received a couple of curious glances but no flickers of interest as the team passed me with their gear. "Jerry, is Ben frcc to go?"

He nodded. "I've got enough preliminary information from Ben, but I'll call him later so he can make a statement. You, too, Andi."

Ben said, "The produce truck usually gets here around seven. I can wait here for them."

"I'll let them know the restaurant is closed today. You can go on home." Jerry waved us off. "I'll let you know when you can come back and lock up."

Ben and I stared through the glass doors and into the dining room. When would voices fill this room again, along with the sounds of clanking dinnerware and the ancient jukebox? I reached for Ben's hand and held on tight.

Honey Haggerty. Dead. Murdered. With my free hand, I touched my own throat. Someone had to be strong to hold down the wiry redhead and force watermelon rind down her throat. She'd probably fought hard. I squinted to see past the dining room and into the large opening that exposed the kitchen area. I could glimpse a stainless steel worktable topped with a cutting board. A large watermelon rested on the board and scraps of rind. On the floor, a hand and forearm protruded from behind the stainless steel prep table. Each finger was covered with rhinestone-spangled rings. Even at this short distance, they caught the fluorescent lights above.

"Let's go home." I squeezed Ben's hand. All he did was nod. We started walking to his truck. At the edge of the treetops lining the horizon, the sky started to bloom a faint pink.

"Are you all right?" I asked as we stopped at Ben's truck.

He shrugged. "I can't believe it happened. So many things to take care of. I guess Jerry will let Honey's sister know."

"She has a sister?" Obviously I really didn't know

Honey that well. "I never knew."

Ben nodded. "They don't get along. Honey says all her sister ever did was call her for money, so some years back Honey quit taking her phone calls. But her sister showed up here every week like clockwork, like she wanted to remind Honey they were family." He opened his mouth again, and I waited for him to continue, but he said no more. He acted like he wanted to tell me something more, though.

"A sister. I ate at Honey's enough. How come I never saw her?"

"You probably have. She colored her hair the same shade as Honey's. It's real poufy, too."

"That narrows it down. We have more than a few bottled redheads in the over-fifty set." I couldn't imagine Di and I being at odds. Not like that, anyway. If Di ever needed me or I needed her, we were there for each other. And neither of us ever felt like we took advantage of the other.

"If she shows up at the funeral, I'll point her out to you."

"Okay. Sorry. I didn't mean to sound snappy. It's just the shock of Honey's murder, and it's so early."

"I know. I'm tired, too." The lines around Ben's eyes made him look older. I didn't remember him looking so tired when he was on the road. For longer than we dated, for years, Ben had crisscrossed the lower forty-eight but always managed to find his way back to Greenburg and me. Sure, he'd get tired while driving long hauls for a thousand miles or so, but Ben always called that a "good tired." Now that he'd lived full-time in Greenburg, it seemed like Ben's tired had taken on another character.

"Let's go home. In fact, I won't open my shop today, either." Sometimes we got so busy running to our jobs, it was easy to get lost in work and forget what, or who, really mattered most. Our time with God. Our time with people.

"You don't have to close today."

"But I want to." It was my turn to pull him close, and we clung to each other. But I was worried. I couldn't drag his unspoken words out of him, and I knew Ben would talk when he was ready. Trouble was, what wasn't he telling me?

I picked up the Wednesday afternoon edition of the *Greenburg Dispatch* and set down my cup of tea. Someone had literally stopped the presses, inserted the news of Honey's murder, and restarted them in a hurry. The article merely stated that Honey had been found dead at her restaurant, and that foul play was suspected. It even had some pictures of Honey's Place over the years, including a few of her pies and a picture of a much younger Honey cutting the ribbon to open the restaurant about thirty years ago.

We'll sure miss Honey, and we'll miss her home cooking. Let's hope that whoever takes over her restaurant keeps up her tradition of stick-to-your ribs dining. And let's hope that the Greenburg Police Department swiftly brings Honey's killer to justice.

Which goes to show you how quickly the importance of news changes. The discovery of the remains in our watermelon field took up two paragraphs at the bottom of the front page. Considering I'd been worried about public scrutiny and gawkers at our watermelon field, I couldn't complain. Tears pricked my eyes, though. I hadn't wanted attention to shift like this. Not with someone else's death. *Oh, Honey, all the times I could have been your friend instead of being jealous.*

I placed the newspaper on the coffee table and listened to the sound of the shower running. Ben had had a good nap once we'd returned home from Honey's Place. After I turned off the phone ringer, that is. A Memphis television station called, but I ignored the voice on the answering machine.

Now, Ben would be under investigation, besides a few other people. Sure, Ben had no motive, but Jerry had to do his job. I had to make another suspect list, so I reached for my notepad. I would continue my investigation into the remains and the possibility they were my aunt Jewel—I hadn't dared to ask Jerry about the progress on identifying the remains, not when a fresher body had presented itself. But I needed to think about Honey's murder. Ben's reputation was at stake.

If Honey had known anything about my aunt Jewel's disappearance, that knowledge was lost forever. I yanked my focus back to Honey. Her list was easier to write. I left off Ben, of course. There was that cook Honey'd fired, the one she said had stolen from her. Gabe Davis. And the alleged affair with Roland Thacker. I hated putting Roland on the list, especially since the suspicion was based on gossip, but I did it anyway. Jerry had a right to know, and if nothing came of it, then fine.

And what about that sister Ben had mentioned? I'd ask Ben if he knew more about her. Maybe Jerry would know. Plus, Honey and Junker Joe had been arguing last night. They did that a lot even while they really seemed to love each other. But Junker Joe went on my list, too. What was it she wouldn't change her mind about?

I didn't want fingers pointed at Ben, but I didn't want to go out of my way to point them at anyone else. Did blind Justice ever peek around her blindfold? I didn't think I could have ever been a lawyer.

Ben appeared in the doorway. "Now that feels better." He stifled a yawn with one hand as he rubbed his head with a towel. "I didn't think I could sleep, but somehow I did."

"I knew you needed the sleep." I picked up the paper. "Here's the front page."

"I don't want to read it." Ben sank onto the couch, and I snuggled closer to him. "I know enough already."

"Well, I decided I'm going to add to the care package for the Davis family. If his wife is chasing a toddler, I bet she'd love some pampering. So I'm making her a soap and bath salts gift basket. Besides bringing some groceries." I inhaled deeply. Ben smelled of soap, and I wouldn't share him with anyone.

"That's why I love you so much. You're thinking of Gabe's wife, when all some people would have seen yesterday was a wild man. Today they're thinking he's a murderer."

He continued speaking as he sipped the coffee I'd handed him. "Jerry has let the state police know, in case Gabe's running. I don't know if he ever went home last night. He works part-time as a groundskeeper at the community college in Selmer. I wanted Honey to give him another chance, but she said no go."

"And then as far as suspects there's also. . ." I stopped myself.

"There's. . . ?"

"I was thinking of another suspect, but it's not really credible. Roland Thacker."

"Mm-hmm." Ben stared hard at the fireplace. "The weather's too humid to light a fire. I think the sun might come out for a while today."

"What's that 'mm-hmm' all about? Do you know something I don't?"

Ben shook his head. "Nothing, really. You're right. No one's a suspect because of mere rumors. Honey sure had a magnetism about her. Either you were attracted to her or she repulsed you."

That made me laugh. "Ben!"

"I'm serious, she did. And she'd admit that."

"You. . .you weren't attracted to her, were you?" My heart thudded. Surely not.

"Like my daddy always said, why go out for a burger when you have prime rib at home?" He leaned in to kiss me, and this made me shove thoughts of murderers and motives out of my head for the rest of the afternoon.

My Jeep passed through the gateway to Shady Pines mobile home park on the south end of town. I squinted at the numbers on the homes nestled among trees. Not bad. A little too close for me, though. I liked our country space just fine.

I found 17 Briar Patch, a narrow white trailer with a four-door sedan parked in front on a concrete slab. The other side of the slab was vacant, but a grease spot showed where another vehicle usually parked. Someone had planted rose bushes along the side of the trailer, and two lawn chairs and a barbecue grill sat on the deck. I pulled the sack of groceries and the gift basket off the front seat and climbed the stairs.

When I rang the doorbell, footsteps approached the door from inside. "I don't want to talk, if you're a reporter."

"It's—it's Andi Hartley. My husband, Ben, worked with Gabe at Honey's."

A wisp of a girl pulled open the door. She barely looked eighteen but held a little girl with round brown eyes on her hip. "Hi. Come on in. I'm, um, Maryann." I entered a living room that smelled faintly of cigarette smoke.

"I brought a few things. I know with your husband losing his job, it's probably been hard. And I brought something for you, too." I placed the basket of soaps and sack of groceries on the nearby dinette table.

Maryann set her little girl down, and the toddler ran to a Dora the Explorer table in the corner. "That's so sweet of you. It's been awhile since anything good has happened to us."

"Well, Ben said he tried to get Gabe's job back for him, but Honey wouldn't listen."

Her brow furrowed. "And now that Honey's been murdered, I just know things will go from bad to worse for us. But Gabe wouldn't do anything like that. Sure, he got mad, but what guy wouldn't?"

"Where is he?"

Maryann shook her head. "I don't know. He came home late last night. The storm kept me up, and Zoë couldn't sleep either. Gabe was scared."

"What happened?"

"He said he was in big trouble, and he had to go. He. . .he went by the restaurant, late, because he wanted to beg one last time for his job back. And. . ."

"Was she already dead?"

"I don't know." Maryann grabbed a tissue and dabbed at her eyes. "Then he packed a few clothes, said he would let me know he was okay."

"You need to talk to my brother-in-law, Jerry Hartley."

"I did. And they're still trying to find Gabe to bring him in for questioning." Maryann shuddered. "I don't know what I'd do if I lost him."

"What about your family?"

"They didn't want me to marry him, but then I found out I was going to have Zoë, and so. . ." She rose and went to the kitchen sink and stared out the window. "Just go. Please. Thanks for thinking of us. I appreciate it. But go."

"I think my husband might be in trouble, too. He's the one who found her."

Maryann whirled to face me. "But he didn't explode at her in front of a room full of people."

I stood, making sure the sack of groceries didn't tumble on its side. "I'm just sayin' Gabe's not the only suspect. There's more than him."

"But he's at the top of the list. And look, if both our men might be in trouble, we probably don't need to be talkin' to each other."

"Well, if you need anything, call us anyway. Or come by the restaurant. Ben won't turn you away."

Maryann dismissed me by looking out the kitchen window once more.

I went back to the Jeep and climbed into the driver's side. A small white box containing a home pregnancy test rested on the passenger seat. I had no idea what Maryann was going through. Some parents would do anything for their children. I didn't know how that felt, and I wasn't sure if I wanted to know that desperation. Shoving those thoughts aside, I headed home.

Drew, my brother-in-law's cousin and a lawyer, gave us a phone consultation on Thursday night about Ben's situation. We sat in the living room. After my conversation with Maryann Davis the other day, I was determined to do all we could to take Ben's name off the suspect list as soon as possible.

"It's not likely that you'll be charged with a crime or even be terribly high on the list of suspects, at this point." Drew's voice sounded tinny over the speaker phone.

"But what about questioning?" Ben asked. "I gave a statement about the night of the crime. Isn't that enough? Or will they keep asking me questions even though I've already told them everything I know about the night of the murder?"

"Ben, they can question you as many times as they feel they need to. What I'd suggest, and this is just a suggestion, is that you secure an attorney to be present whenever you meet with the police. It's not a necessity—you haven't been mirandized or anything—but for your own peace of mind, an attorney can step in if he or she feels that the questioning crosses the line to self-incriminating."

I squeezed Ben's hand and murmured, "I think we need to hire Drew. Even if we have to pull from our savings, I want him available if. . ."

Ben squeezed my hand in response. "Drew, can we hire you? Just in case. You know Jerry and I are family, and I don't want anyone saying he's giving me favors. If anything, I might be under more scrutiny because Jerry *is* my brother."

"Not a problem. Come by the office, and we'll get the paperwork started."

I could see Ben's features relax. He still didn't meet my eyes.

We ended the call, and I asked, "Ben, are you all right?"

"I'm nervous."

"It's going to be okay." *Look at me.* "We'll get through this together. You don't have anything to be nervous about."

Even with Drew's reassuring words, I couldn't slow my heartbeat at the idea of Ben getting hauled in for questioning. Not that Jerry would do any hauling in, but that the DA, being thorough, would be extra aggressive in his investigation. And I sure hoped nothing came to light that would throw undue suspicion in Ben's direction.

Our phone rang less than a week later, promptly at eight in the morning. I was busy getting ready to head out to open the shop. Ben met me in our bedroom and took the call. He still wasn't sure what to do about the restaurant—he had started opening for breakfast and lunch only, while still waiting to hear from Honey's lawyer about her will. He had already assured the rest of the staff they still had jobs. For the moment. The employees had somehow automatically looked to Ben for guidance, but that didn't surprise me. Ben inspired confidence in people. I know he always settled me down in stressful moments. But now Ben had his own stress to battle. Having Drew as our advocate and legal advisor gave both of us some peace of mind. We thanked God for good family connections.

"Well, that was Honey's lawyer, Robert Robertson, on the phone," Ben said. "He wants us to come to his office at ten."

"Oh, you've *got* to be kidding me. Robert Robertson is her lawyer?" This just got better and better. I'd made a fool of myself last summer in his office while investigating Charla Thacker's death, who just happened to be his fiancée. "Do I need to be there? I wasn't Honey's employee or anything."

"You do. He specifically said that Benjamin and Andromeda Hartley needed to be present."

"Present?"

"For the reading of the will."

"I guess I won't be opening the store until after lunch, then." I put the toothpaste back into the medicine cabinet and tried not to fidget. I should have used the bathroom first thing, but I didn't want to pull out the pregnancy test in front of Ben. What if he was disappointed at the result? Now I really had to go, and he hovered by the bathroom door.

"No hurry. In fact, I'm going to get another cup of coffee and read the paper." Ben kissed my cheek before he left.

Now I turned my attention back to the test and read the directions. My heart pounded. I didn't think I was pregnant. I'd waited nearly a week, and I still had no symptoms other than queasiness some mornings. None of the telltale signs of early pregnancy. But other women always volunteered plenty of information, so I knew some expectant mothers had virtually no symptoms.

Five minutes later I'd followed the directions on the package and was making our bed. I picked up a few of Ben's wayward dirty socks and plunked them in the hamper. The digital alarm clock flashed another minute ahead. Time to see. One line, or two?

I almost knocked the little plastic stick into the trash can but managed to pick it up. One line. I sank onto the closed toilet seat. Relieved or disappointed, I didn't know.

"She left us *what*?" I didn't care that my voice squeaked. Ben swallowed hard and looked at me.

"Honey's Place, including the property and building and all its contents." Robert Robertson's voice sounded as if he were addressing a child.

I couldn't breathe. "But. . ." I flung a glance at Ben, who cleared his throat before he spoke.

"Thank you for letting us know. We sure didn't expect that." Ben fumbled with his collar and an imaginary tie. "What do we do now?"

Robert picked up his phone. "Business as usual. It wouldn't surprise me, though, if someone from her family comes forward to contest the will. Ms. Haggerty made this change to her will about six weeks ago. Here's a note she left, explaining her decision. Notarized, also. I think her wishes are very clear, and her family won't have much grounds to contest." Then he spoke into the phone receiver. "Suzie? I need you to copy Ms. Haggerty's will."

We told him good-bye, received the sealed note from Honey, our copy of the will, and left. Ben opened my door for me before climbing into the truck.

"What just happened?"

I rubbed my forehead. "I don't know whether to laugh or cry." One business was hard enough to run, but to own one of Greenburg's best-known restaurants? "Let's read the letter. What on earth made her leave the place to us?"

Honey's scrawl explained:

"If you're reading this, then the worst has happened and nobody's eating any more of my pies." My throat caught. The flame-haired woman had somehow wiggled her way into a corner of my heart, but I'd never tried to get close to her. *"Ben, I never had much use for my own family, and in the months you've worked for me you showed you earned a place as my kin. Andi-girl, you've got a good hardworking man there who loves you. . ."*

Here my voice quavered. Honey had been lonely, and her larger-than-life manner wasn't showing off. It was a cry to be loved and wanted. The attention seeking, the winks and flirts. All cries. I should have given her a chance.

Ben brushed a tear from my cheek. "You okay?"

I nodded. "She was so lonely, and I never really tried to get to know her. I never dreamed she thought so much of you. . .of us. . ."

"Is that all in the note?" He leaned closer, and his closeness made me want to lean against him and cherish every heartbeat.

"No, there's more: '. . .you've got a good hardworking man there who loves you. Don't be afraid. Start that family. My little hole-in-the-wall diner isn't much, but I hope it gives you two the start of a better way of life.*

I've got too many regrets to name. I just pray this one act makes up for what I've done in the past. Sincerely, Harriet Haggerty."

"I didn't know her real name was Harriet." Ben rubbed his eyes and looked out the window. "Didn't know a lot of things about her."

"She sounds like she carried a heavy load." I ran my finger over the vivid strokes of the pen. "I wonder what she regretted." I scanned the passersby outside. Life had gone on without Honey, as it does when any of us leaves this life. But she left a hole. And someone had made sure of that.

First Aunt Jewel, now Honey. A figure emerged from Greenburg's Town Hall. Roland Thacker, with a spring in his step I hadn't seen, well, ever. He grinned as he talked on his cell phone. I rolled my window down as he passed in front of the truck.

"Yes, Cynthia, I'll meet you for lunch. You're right. This is a new start, for both of us." His glance flicked in my direction and a shadow crossed his face briefly, then he smiled at his wife's words and continued on his way.

Roland stood to gain something by Honey's death, if only a little peace of mind, if Vivian Delane's rumor was true. But if some in town already knew the rumor, then what else did he have to lose? I closed my eyes. If the affair had continued. . .

"What's going on in that gorgeous head of yours?" Ben nudged me before he started the truck.

"Thinking about who would stand to benefit from Honey's death." I put up a mental roadblock about

Roland Thacker. A new start for Roland. No more reminders of guilt, perhaps?

We backed out of the parking space and continued down Main Street. I could tell Ben's mind was turning in circles, so I kept silent while he drove.

"Well," he continued, "the cold hard reality would point to us. We certainly benefited from her death."

"We didn't know about this ahead of time, even if the change was in the last few weeks. Wait. . .is that what she wanted to talk to us about the morning she was killed?"

Ben shrugged. "Sort of."

"You *knew*?" The truck hit a bump, and I gripped the armrest. "That's kind of big news to sit on for weeks." I shut my mouth after that, not realizing till then how it felt to love someone and simultaneously want to strangle them. No, not strangle. Not after what had happened to Honey.

His jaw pulsed. "I didn't *know*. Not for sure. I figured something was up. She was talking about the future a lot. About families. Why she'd never gotten married. How you and I needed to work on a family. How she wanted to make sure we were taken care of." His face flushed at this.

"Y'all talked about a lot, then."

"About you and me. Believe it or not, you really impressed her, startin' Tennessee River Soaps. Said you had a lot of backbone, and she liked that. Especially around here, in a town like this."

We arrived at my store, where work waited for me and I wouldn't have time to think of murderers.

"Wow," was all I could say. Now I knew I had to try to find her murderer. Ben didn't need to be put under more scrutiny, and the revelation of Honey's will would do just that. Once he informed the employees and filed more paperwork, the news would spread like a flash fire.

"I need to get to the restaurant. Might as well let the staff know." Ben had settled into his role as leader at Honey's Place. Esther didn't seem too thrilled about him telling her what to do, although the older waitress had listened to Honey most of the time without a problem.

"Does Jerry know yet? If he does, you know he's going to ask you more questions." I shivered despite the humidity and midday sun outside. "I don't like it, Ben, not one bit. And I wish you'd told me about what you suspected."

"I had no way of knowing for sure. You knowin' about my suspicions wouldn't have made much difference, would it?"

"No. You're right."

"What's that?" Ben cupped his ear. "Did I hear. . . ?"

"I said, you're right." My feathers sure stood up on end, and I didn't want to part that way.

He kissed me before I left the truck. "I'm just playin', baby. I love you."

"I love you, too. Don't forget to pick me up at five. Remember, we're having dinner at my parents' tonight."

Ben slapped his forehead. "Aw, and I gave Jonas the night off." Jonas was another of Honey's trusty crew. He'd worked for years on the Mississippi River and only in the past five years had started to work for Honey. Word also had it that he'd lost his wife years ago and now was helping his daughter raise her children alone as well.

Ben sure was batting a thousand today. Men. I'd told him several times we were having dinner at Momma and Daddy's tonight. "I can get Di to pick me up."

"No, I can cut out for a while."

Ben let me out at Tennessee River Soaps and sped off in the direction of Honey's. I turned and trudged to my back door. Good thing I'd brought my notepad with me today. Another attempt to stay organized courtesy of Di. I flipped to the pages for Aunt Jewel and for Honey.

While the air conditioner did its work and my Internet orders downloaded, I scanned my list. Or lists. Aunt Jewel and Honey had known each other. Was there a link between the past and the present? I drew a line between Honey and Aunt Jewel on my list, then added a question mark. How odd, to find part of a skeleton, and once that news flew around, the next day Honey ended up dead. If, and I didn't think it was a big if, the remains were Aunt Jewel's, then the connection between the two deaths couldn't be just quirky timing. Momma would know. And tonight I'd try to get some answers out of her.

7

Well, the Lord's sure smiled on you and Ben." Momma put another plate of biscuits on the table in front of me. I passed on the biscuits. *To her who hath shall be given more.* I sure didn't want the benefits of that abundance on the table to show up on my hips.

The seat next to me remained empty, and I tried not to think about that too much. "It sure was a surprise to me. I run circles trying to keep up with Tennessee River Soaps. And I only have one employee. Part-time, at that."

"Does that mean we can get free burgers?" asked twelve-year-old Stevie.

"Um, that I don't know. I'll have to ask Ben." Stevie's question made me smile. Somehow a biscuit ended up on my plate and my hand reached of its own accord for the butter. Reflex eating. Not good. "But I bet we can work something out."

"Cool!"

My nephews piled their plates high, except for vegetables. Di snatched the bowl of broccoli topped with melted cheese and gave them each a generous spoonful. Stevie told her he didn't care for broccoli.

Daddy was busy showing Momma some travel trailer brochures, and Taylor started negotiating with Di about how much of his broccoli he had to eat. My sister's eyes looked tired.

"Di. . .are you okay?"

She glanced at my brother-in-law before answering. "We've had a lot going on lately. Honey, could you tell them?"

"I got a promotion and, uh, we're moving to Jackson." He tousled Taylor's hair. "We told the boys we'd find a house with a big yard so we can have a dog."

Di smiled, and I recognized its tacked-on appearance. "I'm happy for Steve. He's worked so hard, and this will let him be home on weekends. We can always come back to visit. An hour isn't a long drive."

I tried to swallow around the lump in my throat. The biscuit on my plate was safe from ending up in my stomach. "Wow. How soon?"

"We. . .we'd like to find a house before school starts."

Four weeks, max. Momma stood up so fast, she nearly turned her chair over. "I'll put on some decaf, and we can all have a cup with some of the wonderful chocolate applesauce cake Diana brought."

Great. We could all stress-eat together. Now wasn't the time to pry information out of Momma about Aunt Jewel and Honey. I helped Momma clear the table. Before long the coffee gurgled in the pot, and I sure wanted a cup.

Someone banged on the back door, so Momma crossed through the laundry room to answer it. Stevie made a remark about Grandma not having a dishwasher, and Di countered they had plenty of dishwashers sitting around the dining table. Momma returned, with Jerry following. He turned his hat over in his hands and nodded his head.

"I'm sorry to interrupt your family dinner."

"Don't lose sleep over it, Jerry," my dad said. "We're about to have dessert. Grab the chair by Andi." I seemed to have lots of empty chairs next to me lately.

"Hey, Andi." Jerry nodded at me. "Thank you for the offer, but I can't stay. But I wanted to stop by and tell y'all in person. Good thing everyone's here, so you can all find out at the same time. Heard back about those dental records."

It felt like someone had pulled a plug and the air whistled out of the room.

"Spit it out, then." Daddy shifted in his chair and stared Jerry in the eye.

"Darlin'," Momma chided. "We've known Jerry since he ran around in braces and skinned his knee on the road goin' past the house. But he's the law. We've got to show him a little respect."

"I know, I know. Sorry. It's just been hard to sleep around here lately."

"The body in your field, Andi. . ." Jerry swallowed hard. He stared at the floor, then glanced at me, then at the floor.

"It's Aunt Jewel," I said. Momma sank onto her chair.

"You're right." Jerry looked apologetic. "I'm glad we found out so quickly, for your sakes."

"Me, too." Momma's voice was barely a whisper. "Someone needs to tell your Papaw, girls. I don't think I can."

Di murmured quietly, explaining to the boys.

Steve took her hand. Momma moved over to Daddy, who pulled her onto his lap. I wanted Ben's closeness. I shouldn't have felt alone, here with my parents, sister, and the rest of the gang.

"I can tell Papaw." My voice squeaked in my ears. Confirmation of my suspicion didn't console me much.

Momma nodded, but I didn't think she really heard me. "Thank you, Jerry. I appreciate you coming by. Sure you don't want that slice of cake to take home for later?"

"No, but thank you again, Mrs. Clark. Uh, I can have her sent to Warner's when we're done, if you want. Then you can call them to make arrangements."

Another nod from Momma. "But how did she die? Can they tell that from. . .from what's left?" She frowned and reached for a napkin.

"The medical examiner is still performing tests on samples from the bones, and we're still waiting to hear back on the final reports." Jerry touched Momma's shoulder. "I tell you what. I'm praying they find some answers for you. Not many families get the answers they want, or any that'll satisfy."

"We appreciate what you're doing, Jerry," Daddy said.

With another nod to me, Jerry left the way he came, and Di's luscious cake was left on the table with all of us gawking at it.

"Let's have some cake." Momma kissed Daddy on his forehead and went to get some clean plates.

Di and I stared at each other. Di finally spoke.

"Momma, it's so sad."

Momma whirled with a stack of plates and faced us. "I mourned her a long time ago. I lost her before she disappeared. Ran with a different crowd of friends. Maybe that's why Honey Haggerty gave y'all that restaurant. She and your aunt. . ."

I took the plates from Momma's hands and placed them on the table. "What? I know they were a few years apart in age."

"They were always out and about." Momma reached for a knife, bit her lip, and started slicing cake. "Jewel didn't like to be home. It was boring. Our parents were too old to know what fun was, she said. She, Honey, Bobby Johnson, Joe Toms, a few others all ran around." The knife clinked on the plate. I sure hoped it wasn't Di's good china.

"One night Daddy caught Jewel sneakin' out. Oh, but your Papaw had a temper back then. Still does, sometimes. He never liked Bobby, either, and that boy had a temper to match Daddy's." When Momma glanced at Stevie and Taylor, who sat perched on the edge of their seats listening to her, she fell silent.

"It's all right, Momma." Di glanced at Steve. "We've told the boys what we know as best we can."

"Jewel and Bobby were neck-deep, flat-out in love. I don't know why they didn't just get married. Daddy, probably." Momma found the forks and passed them around.

"When Aunt Jewel. . .disappeared, were any of her things missing?" I asked. "Was she trying to leave town?"

"I think some of her clothes were gone, and a

suitcase. My momma and daddy were devastated. I had you, Andromeda, to help me smile. Plus Diana came not long after, needing my attention. My two consolations." Momma blinked hard and reached for a fork.

I dared not ask more. Momma's information had caused more questions to swirl through my mind. Tonight, especially with the boys around, I didn't want to keep dredging up the past. The pain of it lurked in Momma's eyes. Sure, Momma might have mourned her sister years ago, but tonight's confirmation must have made her feel like she'd lost Jewel all over again.

After I managed to eat half a slice of cake, Di and Steve decided to leave, and they offered to drop me by the house. I could see the glow of the Honey's Place sign as we passed the side street off downtown. A few cars remained in the parking lot, and I glimpsed the hood of Ben's truck.

"I'm sorry we had to spring the news about our move at supper tonight." Di looked over her shoulder from the front passenger seat. "We were plannin' on tellin' y'all before one of the boys did. If we'd have known Jerry was coming by, I don't think we would have said anything to Momma." She smiled fondly at Taylor, who leaned back in the seat, eyes closed, mouth gaping in sleep.

"That's all right. It was a lot to hear at once."

"We can both call Momma tomorrow to see how she's doing. I imagine she'll want to plan a funeral."

"Probably. First Honey, and now this." I shook my head. Steve turned the van, and we entered our driveway. Watermelons studded the field. Oh, Aunt

Jewel. And Honey.

After a hug and a wave, they left me opening my own back door. Spot zoomed to meet me when I stepped inside the kitchen, and I closed the door before she got any ideas about prowling in the field that night. No more surprises.

Papaw had a temper, especially back then. But he wouldn't have killed Aunt Jewel for trying to leave, would he? I'd seen a sibling kill another last summer. Sometimes you just didn't know family well enough. Now I understood Roland Thacker's disbelief that one of his daughters could have murdered the other.

Spot mewed for some food, so I filled her dish while she pranced around the kitchen. Honey said that Ben and I ought to start our family. Tonight I missed him more than ever, and I blamed Honey for it, dead though she was. He had taken the responsibility of running the restaurant seriously, I knew, and I couldn't fault him for that. If only he had a different job, with regular hours.

Then I recalled Ben hadn't shared his suspicions with me about Honey leaving us the restaurant. Her letter remained tucked in my purse where I'd put it after closing the store that afternoon.

I retrieved the letter and scanned it once more. *I've got too many regrets to name. I just pray this one act makes up for what I've done in the past.*

Honey, what did you do?

8

Thanks to Honey, I had my responsibilities for the Watermelon Festival to keep me busy. I spent the next morning at the shop, making phone calls to other committee members and haggling over themed booths proposed by various vendors. No, we didn't want inflatable swords in every color of the rainbow or other county fair junk.

The door clanged open, and in came Vivian Delane. I hung up the phone. "Hi, it's good to see you."

"You, too." She ran one of her manicured fingernails along a display of soaps then picked one up and sniffed it. "You haven't been by the gym in a while."

"Oh, well, um. . ." I already felt like I'd put on five pounds with her just walking into the store. "It's been pretty stressful around here lately. I've had a lot to do with work, my family situation, the Watermelon Festival."

"I see. You know, exercise can help ease stress. Which is why I do so much of it." Vivian grinned then continued her elegant prowl around the shop. "Oh, how lovely. Lavender. I'm making gift baskets. Several birthdays in my family are coming up this fall and I want to get ahead."

The woman was in better shape than I'd ever been, and now she just showed she was better organized, too. "Super. I can help you put some collections together."

Twenty minutes later she had three piles of

coordinating soap products in Lavender Luxury, Wily Watermelon, and Gardenia Frenzy. The last scent I assured her would be ideal for her teenage niece starting college. Sweet, with a hint of spice. Sadie had helped me come up with that scent while we experimented one rainy afternoon earlier in the summer.

"I can't believe she's already out of high school. Seemed only months ago I was helpin' my sister burp and feed the little bundle." Vivian sighed. "Curtis and I always wanted children, but I guess I ended up experiencing parenthood through my sister."

"Your niece must have been fun to spoil. I have nephews, and I'm not sure how to handle them sometimes." I glanced at the clock. Sadie was due to arrive around two o'clock to work because I had a laundry monster threatening to invade the kitchen if I didn't deal with it.

Vivian nodded and focused on the soap covering the counter. Her long lashes blinked. "She was. What about you? You don't have kids yet, do you?"

"No, not yet." I bit my lip. "Eventually. Someday."

"Oh, that's what Curtis and I always said. Until we tried. And then I found out I couldn't have children. Ever." Her lips twisted into a wistful smile. "Take my word for it. Don't put off a family, sayin' you will when you can afford it."

Her tone made me pause. Vivian, sharing from her heart? She didn't seem like the sharing kind. "Thanks for telling me that. You've given me some things to think about."

"Well, you're welcome." She fumbled with her wallet

and pulled out a one-hundred-dollar bill as I totaled her purchase. "Don't know what got into me. This place is so peaceful. Relaxin'."

"I'm glad you like it." I carefully wrapped her purchases. "Come back anytime."

As I watched Vivian leave, I thought about the softer side of her that I'd just witnessed. She reminded me of the trainer on that weight loss reality show on TV. She could always get an extra dozen crunches or leg lifts out of a client.

I was relieved she didn't ask about the body in the field. Evidently the news had been overshadowed some by Honey's death. Aunt Jewel's disappearance had been overshadowed, too, Momma had told me earlier that morning. But the news that temporarily helped sell a few newspapers years ago still remained important to our family thirty years later.

I frowned at the dirty socks, grease-stained T-shirts, and multiple pairs of jeans. And that was just Ben's stack of work clothes. He'd made a pointed remark last night about having only one pair of clean socks left in his drawer. He changed clothes more than anyone I ever knew, and that counted women, too. He'd spend twelve or more hours at the restaurant, then come home and shower and change again before going outside to hammer and nail on his latest project, if time allowed. Multiply that by six days, and I had the makings of a Rocky Mountain right here in Tennessee. And that didn't even count his workout clothes. Married life really had no glamour when it came down to everyday stuff like laundry or planning meals.

Speaking of which, I dared not serve leftovers again tonight. Honey used to send extra food home with Ben quite often, but I really needed to try to pick up a cookbook. I knew Ben didn't want to come home to have to cook again.

"Romance is highly overrated," I said to the jug of detergent.

"Baby, I'm home." My Prince Charming came through the back door, smelling like french fries and hamburgers. "I brought us a late lunch. Or early supper if you want to call it that."

"Wow, thanks." How would I ever learn to cook, with Ben bringing food home? "You didn't have to. I was going to throw something together." Never mind that our stainless steel Crock-Pot was still in the box in the guest bedroom, along with a copy of *Fast Fix-It Meals* from Diana.

"I've got some news. The Chamber of Commerce contacted me about assuming Honey's membership. Guess I'll be rubbing elbows with the rest of the crowd." He gave me a little-boy grin. "Maybe I should get a tie."

"Right!" I tried not to snort. "Don't get a tie. It's not, um, you."

"Roland Thacker and a few other businessmen have asked me to join them for a supper meeting at the Riverfront Grille."

"Wow, now that's something." The laundry

couldn't wash itself, so I quit stalling. I snapped the water temperature to hot and started tossing socks and other whites into the washer. "What's the meeting about?"

Ben removed his shirt, which bore the brunt of his labors that day. "They want to give me a few business pointers. They know I'm new to running a business and want Honey's Place to stay afloat."

"I wonder if any of them have their eye on it." I closed the washer lid and turned to face Ben. "What if they want the restaurant to go under, and by bailing you out, they make it look like they're doing you a favor?"

"Don't be so suspicious. The way they put it, Honey's Place benefits the town. We employ ten Greenburg residents and provide good competition for other restaurants. Plus great down-home cooking." Ben took my hands. "The restaurant is a great opportunity for us. Tonight I get to do some detective work, too."

"What do you mean?"

"I asked Honey's accountant to print out the last year's worth of transactions, just so I can see where we are. Honey always handled the books herself. Anyway, I noticed somethin' strange. For the last five months, she made large cash deposits once a month. For the same amount each time."

"Why's that strange?"

"Her receipt book in her office shows they were received from 'a debtor.' A thousand dollars a month."

The words slammed into me despite my doldrums.

"Was it a business arrangement?"

Ben shrugged. "I have no idea. I can't find papers or anything showing she had a deal going on with anyone."

"What if she knew a secret and was blackmailing someone, or felt they owed her something? Hmm. Roland couldn't stand Honey. Maybe she was hitting him in the wallet every month because of the past. If he was just payin' back a loan, he'd make sure it had a paper trail. But those deposits were cash. And someone like Roland doesn't ask for loans. Not that way." The whole thing smacked of a payoff.

"That's why I'm going to dinner with them. I don't think I'll ask him outright if they had financial dealings."

I bit my lip. "You think I can go, too?"

"Well, uh, they didn't say anything about bringin' wives. Now don't go lookin' sad."

That figured. Another dinner for one and a CSI rerun. "I. . .I don't like that you're gone so much." I detested the quaver in my voice. "I thought for a while your job at Honey's was a good thing. We're content, our bills are paid. We paid for the house as we went along building it. But I feel like you're on the road again, and I'm left with reminders of you while you're gone."

Ben pulled me close, and I caught another whiff of grill. "Shhh. . .I'm here now. Anytime you want to see me at the restaurant, you can come by. You know that. And I promise, whatever Roland tells me, I'll tell you and we can figure it out together."

That wasn't what I meant, but I could try. He sure

supported me when Tennessee River Soaps first opened, and I knew deep down he was probably afraid of failing. The news about Honey's accounts piqued my interest, even as I clung to Ben.

"Okay," I murmured into his shoulder. The ringing phone called me to the kitchen.

"Momma." Two calls from her in the space of six hours, a record for her.

"I just heard from Jerry again. He had more information from the coroner about Jewel. Somethin' he couldn't share last night in front of the kids, he said."

"What's that?"

"Jerry said Jewel had been strangled."

I entered the police station, bypassing Fleta at the desk. She looked a little annoyed at my ignoring her. Jerry was seated behind his desk, and I could see him through the glass windows of his inner sanctum. Ben had left to swing by the restaurant before meeting the other businessmen for supper, so I figured I'd see if Jerry could tell me more about Aunt Jewel.

"Jerry, Momma just called me. What's going on about my aunt Jewel?"

He sighed, looking ten years older than he really was. "Your aunt's case is now a homicide. Unfortunately, they can only do so much with the current case going on."

"You mean Honey's."

Jerry nodded. "Your aunt's case won't be ignored."

"I'm sure, since there's no statute of limitations on murder."

"You're right, there's not."

"What about Gabe Davis? Did you find him yet?"

Jerry shook his head. "No news in that department."

"Well, as far as Aunt Jewel's case is concerned, I'll do what I can to help." I meant it as a promise to both Jerry and to Aunt Jewel. "If I find anything out, you'll be the first to know."

"Do you know anything helpful about your aunt Jewel? Your momma's not the most forthcoming woman."

"My mother said there was a guy, a Bobby Johnson. He and Jewel were in love. He had a temper. So did my Papaw, who didn't approve of them seeing each other."

"Your Papaw, you say? How's his mind holding up?"

"Momma says he has good days and bad days. I'm going to visit him tomorrow. What do you think about having someone meet me there? Maybe he'll remember something about back then."

"It's worth a shot." Jerry rubbed his chin. "I want to have someone out there to talk to him while someone from the family is there. If you'd rather not be there when we talk to him, maybe your mother would come to the nursing home?"

"It's okay. I'll be there. Momma's got enough to worry about right now. I'm planning on being there first thing in the morning, say, around nine, before I open my shop."

"I'll make sure someone meets you there."

9

The CSI rerun ended, and I'd dozed off. So much for learning the solution to the team's case. I shifted from my awkward sprawl on the love seat. In a huff, Spot hopped from her own lazy position on my legs.

"Sorry, Spotter." She rubbed against my ankles when I sat up. Then I heard the rumble of Ben's truck coming up the driveway, his headlights making a bouncing arc as they passed the windows.

I dashed to the kitchen to make a pot of coffee. If Ben had news about Roland, I wanted to hear it and wouldn't let Ben tell me he was too tired to talk. Not tonight, anyway.

"Back again," he said. "Wow, The Riverfront Grille makes a great rib eye." He enveloped me in a hug and gave me a kiss.

"Stop. I'm jealous. But I made coffee so we can stay up and talk. It's still early." I kissed him back before turning to grab two clean mugs from the dish drainer. "Tell me more than what was on the menu. Who was there?"

"Roland Thacker, old Mr. Forrest who runs the drugstore, and Mitchell McCoy."

"What's he do?"

"He has that new organic health-food café. Oat Grass."

"Oh. Organic health food. In Greenburg?" Why

anyone would try to open an eatery in Greenburg that didn't serve anything deep-fried, I didn't understand. I believed in eating healthy but wasn't so sure how the rest of the population felt.

"Anyway, they were helpful. Said I'd been tossed a loaded plate and wanted to help make sure Honey's Place succeeds."

"Okay, that's nothing new from what we knew before you went to dinner. What about Roland? Did he act weird or anything?" We poured our coffee and sat across the table from each other. This was how I liked it. Us talking and sharing. It reminded me of when we dated, even with him out of town. We always caught up. Until he got the job at the restaurant, that is. I stirred a spoonful of vanilla creamer into my coffee.

"He actually asked me an interesting question." Ben took a sip from his cup. "He wondered how the accounts were, if the receipts have maintained. I told him I'd consulted with the accountant who took care of Honey's records. I told him the business is in the black. Didn't want to embarrass him in front of the others by asking if he'd made those cash payoffs, but I asked if anybody knew about Honey loaning money, because she'd made some rather large cash deposits in regular amounts. Roland sputtered on his iced tea. Nearly spewed it across the table at us. Coughed a lot. The others didn't know, but said I ought to check with her lawyer."

"Did Roland say anything that made you think he knew about any payoffs?"

Ben shook his head. "He plowed through dessert

and paid his part of the check in a hurry."

"You need to let Jerry know. I bet the police have already gotten Honey's financial records." I took his hand. "Vivian Delane believes Honey and Roland had an affair at one time."

"Hmm. . .and maybe this was a payoff for her silence?"

"Could be. But Honey's receipt book might not be proof of anything. Nothing connects Roland to those deposits, even with the antagonism he and Honey showed toward each other. Besides, if the one making those payments was Roland, why ask for payment for silence after all this time?" I shook my head. "I don't know. I still say we let Jerry know."

"We'll figure it out. Together." He turned my hand over and ran his thumb over my palm.

"Together. I like that." What I liked more was Ben was finally home, and I had him all to myself.

———

The front doors of Leisure Lodge Nursing Home closed behind me, shutting out the humid air. Still, the air felt stuffy inside the entry. That, and someone had burned the toast this morning. I stopped at the front desk as a familiar figure emerged from the east wing. Curtis Delane. He gave me half a smile and the briefest nod. His carefully gelled hair wasn't budging in any weather, that was for sure. Someone else had cut out from work that morning, too.

"Andromeda."

"Curtis, hello. I'm, um, visiting my papaw today. Do you have family here?"

"My mother. I try to see her as often as I can."

I nodded. Silence fell between us. Something about nursing homes made people forget how to speak, or if they did speak, their voices rose or lowered to unnatural tones like ours had.

"Well, I'll see you at Shapers, I'm sure." I glanced at the clock and signed my name in the book, notating that Jerry was with me. I'd called the director and explained about Jerry coming to ask Papaw some questions. I didn't want anyone wondering why Greenburg PD had shown up. Curtis continued past the reception desk and headed toward the front doors.

As Curtis exited, someone else entered. Jerry, in uniform. He gave me a nod. "I figured I could take a few minutes." He held up a small cardboard tray with two covered paper cups. "Stopped by Trudy's on the way out of town."

What a sweet brother-in-law. I sure hoped he'd find a sweet lady one day. But then I didn't know of anyone I could picture as a match for him. And this morning I needed to remind myself he acted as police officer today, one conducting an investigation at that.

I accepted the cup he offered me. "Oh, thank you. Let's go see Papaw. I sure hope he's having a good morning and can offer you some helpful information."

"I'll wait and have you introduce me first. That way, maybe he won't be too confused. Sometimes the uniform upsets people."

Jerry and I walked to the wing where Papaw stayed and found his room empty. We tracked him to the tropical-themed dayroom where he sat at a table playing dominoes with two other residents. Evidently Papaw had just lost. He scowled at the other players before rising to his feet and shuffling away from the table. When he caught sight of me, he smiled.

"Lookit who showed up. Andromeda Jean. Come and give your papaw a hug."

This was the Papaw I remembered so well. I hugged him, praying that somehow his mind could stay like this always. He could still hug me like an overeager boa constrictor, and according to Momma, his heart was in good shape, too. Just his mind escaped him at times, and when that happened, no one could reason with him.

Once Papaw released me, we sat at an empty table next to a palm tree mural. "I should've come sooner, but we've been pretty busy."

"I know. Where's my Bertie?"

Nana had been gone for five years. "Um, Papaw. . ."

He frowned like a small child. "Wait, a minute. Wait, wait, wait. I remember now. She's gone."

"You're right." I glanced at Jerry, who joined us at the table. "Papaw, this is Jerry Hartley. He's Greenburg's police chief, and he wants to talk to you."

Papaw's eyes flashed. "It weren't me drivin'. They took my license away, the fools. I still know how to steer."

Jerry quirked a smile as he removed a small voice recorder from his pocket and pushed a button. He and

Ben had the same kind of dimple in their cheeks. "I'm not here about anyone's driving today. I'm here to ask you about your daughter Jewel."

"She's gone, too. I know." Papaw slammed his fist on the table, and I couldn't stop myself from flinching. Our coffee cups jiggled. "Noodle-headed girl. I was ready to padlock her door, runnin' out at all hours with that boyfriend of hers."

"She didn't run away with him," Jerry said. "Your granddaughter here found Jewel's remains in a field just outside town."

I watched Papaw's reaction and took a sip of my coffee. Did he understand his daughter hadn't been just gone for thirty years, but was now confirmed dead, too? He fumbled with his shirt collar, then cracked his knuckles.

"Crazy girl." He clenched and unclenched his fists. "Told me she and that punk were gonna get married. One time she sat me and Bertie down to break it to us gentle. . ."

Papaw paused, and I opened my mouth to speak. Jerry shook his head.

"Weren't nothing gentle about it. I could've strangled that girl for bein' so stupid. About to throw her life away."

Strangled. I sucked in a breath and a leftover whiff of burnt toast. Was he speaking figuratively? Papaw had no way of knowing how Aunt Jewel had died, unless. . . "Jerry, do you have to keep asking him questions like this?"

Jerry pushed a button on the recorder and put it

in his pocket. "Mr. Kincaid, we believe someone killed your daughter. Can you think of who might have wanted to do that? I know she really upset you and your wife, but what about the boyfriend?"

"That Bobby Johnson." Papaw's eyes glistened. A tear streaked from the corner of his eye. "Treated her like she was something he bought and paid for. Like that car he was so fond of waxin'. Her momma tried to tell her. Warn her."

"But she wouldn't listen." I touched Papaw's hand and tried to catch his eye. But he'd drifted away and his focus seemed to be on something thirty years ago. I glanced at Jerry. "Maybe we should go. I think he's tired. And he's got a lot to think about." I couldn't imagine fighting to keep my mind drifting through time.

Jerry and I stood at the same time, but Papaw's hand clamped around my wrist. "Where do you think you're going?" Papaw squinted at my face, then studied my neck. "And what'd you do with that locket? Paid good money for it. Some respect you show us, losing your birthday present."

"It's me, Papaw, Andromeda." *Oh, Papaw.*

"Stop tryin' to pull one over on me. Ran off with that Bobby Johnson, and now ya come crawlin' home. Shoulda taken you over my knee more when you were younger." He stood and started to pace the dayroom. I wondered if I should get a nurse or let him walk it off.

Maybe he'd come out of his moment of confusion if I kept reassuring him. "Ben and I bought Doris Flanders' property, and I found a body in the watermelon field."

He continued to pace as I spoke. "They found out it was Jewel by her dental records. She never left us, Papaw." My heart ached to see him like this. "That's what Jerry and I have been trying to tell you."

"Never left." Papaw sank back onto his chair. "All this time. . .I'm sorry. I thought for a minute. . .I hate gettin' confused."

"Don't worry. It's all right. Jerry is going to find out how she got there. So we'll know what happened."

"That redheaded snip might know, too."

"Honey."

"Harriet Haggerty. More mouth on that woman than common sense inside her." Papaw shook his head. "Pearl, you watch your girls around her. Bad news."

"Papaw. . ." I'd lost him again, even as he sat subdued in his chair. The past had flowed into his mind like a rising tide and become the present. I reached for his hand and felt Jerry's sympathetic gaze. "I'll be careful."

"Gimme a hug before you go. Bring those kids next time, you hear?"

"I'll come back soon." It was my turn to give him a squeeze and kiss his forehead. Jerry and I left the dayroom and headed for the front of the building and the entryway. I didn't even stop at the reception desk to sign us out.

We stopped at Jerry's squad car. My earlier shock at Papaw's words made my own thoughts tumble out. "What's next? I heard as well as you did. He said he could have strangled her. You're probably already thinking like I am. Could Papaw have done this? You know I don't think so, but he has a temper. What if he tried to keep her from leaving, and in a moment of anger. . ." I shook my head and shut my mouth.

"Your papaw is an old man, and I don't think it would be hard to get a doctor to show he's not mentally competent, even if he were put on trial. Looking at the worst case scenario, that is." Jerry leaned on the driver's door and rubbed his chin. "I need to speak to your mother next."

"Jerry, you need to find this Bobby Johnson. Besides Papaw, he ought to know. Wherever he is. What can talking to my momma help?"

"She might remember more than she thinks." Jerry unlocked his car and got inside. "One person at a time. I'm going to talk to everyone around here who still remembers your aunt Jewel." Then he shut the door.

I gave him a wave before heading to my Jeep. "Lord, I'm missing something here. I feel like I'm looking at a giant puzzle that's been tossed on the floor. You see all things and know the past, present, and future." All I could see was Papaw's anger, especially at Aunt Jewel wanting to be with Bobby, and his anger at Bobby. If he did kill Aunt Jewel in a rage and bury her in the field, then filing a missing persons report would be a perfect cover. I hated the very idea, but any investigator would put Papaw up high on the suspect list. Learning about the missing persons report had surprised Momma. I couldn't imagine Papaw *not* telling his family about that. Unless he didn't want to raise more questions from them. My head hurt, and the coffee Jerry had brought had already cooled. I pulled out of the nursing home parking lot.

The road back to Greenburg took me through gently rolling hills covered with majestic pines. The hills looked larger up close, but from a plane they'd probably be mere ripples far below. Did our problems and dilemmas seem that way to God? Mere ripples on the ground? No. Jesus had walked this earth, too, and had seen us up close, with our mountains and rolling hills.

Bobby Johnson. Of course. I needed to find out what I could about him. As far as I knew, the guy had disappeared when Aunt Jewel had. I decided to call Roland Thacker first. If they were all around the same age, maybe he knew what had happened to Aunt Jewel's old boyfriend. Jerry could talk to Momma and whoever else he wanted. But I wasn't about to let Papaw's name be ruined. It couldn't happen. Besides, Greenburg now had two open murder cases that needed solving, and Jerry and the force only had so much time. No doubt Jerry had competence and the best of intentions, but with Honey's murder, I didn't want Aunt Jewel's case to slide to the proverbial back burner. When that happened, pots were forgotten.

Before I lost my nerve, I headed straight to Roland's office. Real estate, investments, and abstract business facts and figures had made Roland a pile of money over the years. He even owned some real estate close to Nashville. No, he definitely wouldn't have needed a loan from Honey Haggerty.

His receptionist greeted me from her desk in the slick, contemporary office decorated in chrome, black, and white. The design definitely didn't encourage visitors to linger but to get their business done and get on with it.

"Mr. Thacker is on the phone right now."

"I can wait. I have a quick question that I need to ask him. It should only take five minutes at the most." I settled onto a black polyresin chair and tried not to slide off. No music to set a mood, just the whine of the computer tower's fan on the reception desk.

It wasn't quite the lion's den, but Roland emerged from his office a few minutes later and my palms started to sweat. "Mrs. Hartley. I trust you're doin' well."

"Yes, thank you. I just need five minutes of your time."

"I'm due in Franklin this afternoon. If you don't mind talkin' while I look at a lunch menu? I've got to grab something before I head out of town."

"Not at all." I followed him into an equally stark office. His black leather chair had plenty of cushioning. A black lacquer credenza had a row of white vases on the top. Roland moved to the credenza and took a stack of menus from the top drawer.

"Question away."

"As you know, the remains found in my field belonged to my aunt Jewel. Before she disappeared, her boyfriend was a guy named Bobby Johnson. I'm trying to find him. I think he might know what happened to Aunt Jewel. Did you know him? Or his family?"

Roland studied the menu for Oat Grass. "Hmm. . . Cynthia is always harping about my cholesterol. Should probably order from here today." Either he was being really rude, or he was giving himself time to think of an answer. Or both.

"My brother-in-law calls that place the oats and granola diner."

"Ha. Is that so? He may be right." Roland paused and blew out a breath. "I've got to say that your purpose for visiting today relieved me. I thought you were going to talk about. . .other things."

"I didn't want to intrude too much on your time, but I thought I'd ask around before getting neck-deep in public records."

"Bobby Johnson was a dropout. We didn't really know each other." Roland settled back in his chair. "I think he lived near Doris Flanders. Family had an egg farm. Not much money. Played guitar and sang like a young Elvis. Made us guys want to plow him into the ground sometimes, he had such a big chip on his shoulder. Don't know what Jewel saw in him."

"Any brothers or sisters?"

"Not that I know of."

I could see the conversation was screeching to a halt. "Thanks for your help."

As I rose to leave, he looked up from his menu and picked up his phone. "You guessed about me and Honey. Our, um, indiscretions. But then you're smart. And people talk to you."

"Yes, and I added up some things, but. . ."

"She said she'd tell Cynthia. Ancient history, but Cynthia said she'd leave me if anything ever came up again. I can't afford that, in more ways than one." His brow furrowed, as if reflecting the burden on his soul.

"Why are you telling me this?"

"Because you won't say anything. You know what I've lost already."

"I'm sorry, Roland. In a few years Melinda will be free."

"We're never really free from what we've done in the past." Roland set the phone down. "But Cynthia can't know about Honey."

"It's not my place to tell her." I slung my purse over my shoulder. "Have a good trip to Franklin."

My hands were shaking when I unlocked the Jeep. Poor Roland. *We're never really free from what we've done in the past.* Of course, I'd heard his unspoken wish that I hadn't looked into the real cause of his daughter's death last summer, that I'd refused to believe it was anything more than an unfortunate accidental allergic reaction. Melinda and Roland would always have to live with what they'd done. No peace, unless they accepted forgiveness from God. And even then when God forgives us, some of us can't forgive ourselves.

I glanced at the clock on the dashboard and decided to swing by the post office on the way to the store, where I was due to relieve Sadie at one. Once inside, the air-conditioning provided relief from the humidity. I shivered as I unlocked the box for Tennessee River Soaps. A few supply catalogs—I'd have to check those out and get busy on my fall soap scents, a few bills from vendors. And a plain nine-by-twelve manila envelope. The envelope caught my interest immediately. No return address but postmarked Corinth, Mississippi, about thirty minutes south of Greenburg. Interesting.

Instead of venturing into the heat, I stopped at

a small counter where they kept free envelopes and mailing labels and opened the envelope. A small stack of four-by-six photos slid onto the counter. And a note.

I snatched the photos up. Ben and Honey, at the restaurant. Ben had that goofy look on his face, the one he gets when he's amused and is trying not to laugh. Honey was laughing, an arm around him, one of her hands reaching for his face. The other picture, of which there were several copies at different angles and close-ups, had no people. But it did show Ben's truck and Honey's Harley parked side by side at the Riverbend Inn.

10

Ben's hand held mine in a grip so strong my fingers almost turned white, but I barely felt it. Explanations. I wanted them *now*. The accusing pictures lay on Jerry's desk, next to a duplicate set he'd also received in the mail this morning.

"Who do *you* think sent these?" Jerry slid one set of photos into an evidence bag, along with its manila envelope. "Evidently someone who wants to stir something up. Who would have written that note: '*Ben may say he's innocent, but is he really?*'"

My first thought was Roland Thacker, but I didn't want to go there. I couldn't fathom Roland being able to get pictures like this in a short amount of time. Besides, Roland was too busy to stalk like this.

"Ben, please explain." I'd gotten to Jerry's office at the police station before Ben did. I should have run to Ben, but instead I'd found myself at the police station. Closer than Honey's Place. Plus, I didn't want to stand in the dining room and try to figure out where that picture had been taken. Or succumb to my initial reaction of making a scene and hollering.

"I have an explanation for both." Ben's face flushed as he leaned forward and pointed at the top picture. "See? I've got a smudge of pie on my cheek. Honey was flirting. I mentioned I hated banana cream pie, and she flung some at me. That happened, oh, about two weeks ago. I told her as nice as I could that she needed to back off. And the other one? I let Junker Joe borrow my truck. He needed to pick something up for Honey, a new fryer a couple weeks ago. I think, uh, they made a detour."

"Why didn't you tell me?"

"I didn't think I needed to. We've been all around this when I was on the road."

Thankfully, Jerry was the only witness to this conversation. He seemed to be studying the pictures taken at the hotel room.

I felt Ben's strong, warm hand sending some strength into mine. "I believe you. I do. Because I know you, and I know your heart. And I trust you."

"You know that guys on the road get lots of offers and many don't refuse. But I did. I was always here with you." His words resounded in my ears, and the look in his eyes touched my heart.

"I'm sorry y'all are going through this," Jerry interjected. "But this may help our investigation. We'll send these off to get analyzed."

"Thanks, Jerry." Ben and I still had more to talk about. At least I thought so. "All of this makes me wonder if somehow my aunt's death and Honey's could be related. There's Aunt Jewel's boyfriend, Bobby Johnson."

"Whoa, wait a second." Jerry swiveled his chair, and it squeaked in protest. "You think the cases are related? How's that?"

"The night before I found Aunt Jewel there was a really bad storm that woke me up. I saw someone in our watermelon field. Ben and I ran outside, but whoever it was drove off."

"You should have called me."

"Jerry, it was, like, three in the morning. We didn't see the vehicle very well, and no harm seemed to have been done." I held up my hands. "What would have been the point in calling? Greenburg didn't have any murder cases. But now. . ."

"All right, calm down. You didn't know then. I get that."

"It's because I found Aunt Jewel, and then the next morning, Honey was dead."

"I don't see an immediate connection, at least with the suspects we have at the moment."

I folded my arms across my chest. "Who's at the top of your list?" Jerry glanced at Ben. *No, not Ben.*

"Gabe Davis." Ben nodded. "He hasn't come around the restaurant again since the last day he showed up, angry. The day before Honey died. We're trying to find him. His wife claims she doesn't know where he is. Sounds like he's fleeing, doesn't it?"

Jerry's phone rang, and when he answered it, Fleta's shrill voice carried across the line loud enough for us to hear. "That new doctor is on the phone, the one with the funny name."

"What's she calling about?" Jerry placed his hand over the phone. "Y'all can go," he whispered to us.

"Someone's towing her Beamer, saying they got a complaint about her car blocking the alley behind the offices downtown."

"I'll head over there."

"You aren't sending someone else?"

"No, I'll go." When Fleta started arguing, Jerry told

her that he'd go on whatever calls he felt like.

With that, Ben and I left. The corners of Ben's mouth twitched.

"What?" I smiled at him, despite what had just occurred in Jerry's office. "Did I miss something?"

"I think my little brother has a crush." Ben held open the front door of the police station for me.

"Huh?"

"The new doctor. Dr. Mukherjee."

"Wow." I grinned. "Is she the new woman at church?" I'd noticed the newcomer late in the spring. She looked different for Greenburg, and I overheard her comment one Sunday that she enjoyed participating in the midweek Bible study. I'd missed the study because of all the planning going on for the festival. That, and some nights I was just plain tired.

"I think she's the one. Dr. Bradley added another associate to his practice."

"How'd you find this out?"

"Baby, I run a restaurant."

"I thought you didn't eavesdrop." I couldn't resist taunting him on that one, after the times he'd scolded my overactive imagination when I overhead conversations.

"I don't, but sometimes you can't help but hear things. You can't feel guilty for hearing conversations. It happens all the time." He stopped at his truck, and so did I.

"We seem to be doing this a lot, taking separate vehicles." I rubbed my arms. The image of Honey with one arm slung around Ben still taunted me.

"As long as we wind up at the same place, I don't

mind." Ben pulled me close. "I decided one thing, though. I'm taking the afternoon off."

"Off?"

"Well, we *are* newlyweds." After a quick kiss, he said, "Race you home?"

I ran for the Jeep.

———

Ben lit the grill after we decided to have an early supper. He brushed some sweat from his forehead. "We ought to think about putting in a pool one day."

"Sounds good to me." Clouds had piled up to the west and thunder rumbled in the distance, making me thankful that Ben and Steve had built a covered patio off the back entrance to the house. No rain on our barbecues. "Maybe once we see where we are financially with the restaurant."

"I'm sorry," Ben said as we sat down to eat our delectable Bongo burgers, Ben's signature dish.

"About what?"

"I should have told you about Honey. She only made that one advance with the pie. Really. I think it's a big coincidence that someone had a camera and snapped a picture of us." Ben leaned against one of the awning's support beams. "Unless they kept coming back, trying to find a way to make me look bad."

"Ben, it's done. And I trust you. I would have liked to have known, because it bothered you. I don't think we should keep our struggles from each other, just to spare each other. That's what I'm here for, to support you, like you've supported me. Through the good, the bad, and the really ugly."

"It's different now. On the road, it was like my road life was separate from my life here. I guess I was doin' the same thing with the restaurant. If that makes any sense."

I nodded. "It does. Sort of."

"So you're not mad?"

"I wasn't mad. Disappointed you felt you didn't need to tell me, but now I understand why." Thunder rumbled in the distance. "That picture taken at the restaurant. . .do you remember anyone bringing a camera for a party or something?"

Ben shrugged. "I couldn't tell you for sure when. People bring cameras to the restaurant quite a bit. Birthdays, get-togethers, lunches, you name it. Sometimes for no special reason."

"I still think the deaths are related. Honey's and Aunt Jewel's. I wonder who else might have known Bobby Johnson, Honey, and Aunt Jewel."

"What about Honey's family? I know they weren't close, but we're talkin' at least thirty years ago. They were all a lot younger. I think we could look them up, if Honey named them in her will."

"You're right. I'll go get the copy of her will." I went inside and shivered at the change in temperature. Our copy of Honey's will was tucked neatly in our bill folder.

Ben followed me inside and joined me at the kitchen table. "It's too hot to stay out there. Hope we get rain to cool things off. Not like we need more."

I scanned the paperwork. "Okay. She names a sister, Gretchen Wilkes, who lives in Selmer. Says Gretchen's not getting a dime, thank you very much. She didn't say why. But you already told me about Gretchen always asking for money. Honey also named two cousins, and it's the same thing. Nada. Oh, and that they'd better not expect anything."

"We could always call them and ask."

A few minutes later, Gretchen Wilkes's phone was ringing on the other end of the line. I didn't want to sound like a salesperson. Maybe she wasn't home and I'd be off the hook, no pun intended.

"Hello?" The woman's drawl sounded like it could melt butter.

"Hi, I'm sorry to bother you, but my name is Andromeda Hartley—"

"Whatever you're selling, I'm not wanting. Put me on your no-call list."

"I'm not selling anything." My throat tickled. "I knew your sister, Honey, and I'm trying to find. . .an old friend of hers."

"Won't find any here. She and I ain't talked in almost ten years. Not countin' earlier this year for about five minutes."

"I'm sorry. I have a sister, and I can't imagine how you must feel. But what I'm looking for was a friend she knew about thirty years ago. A Bobby Johnson."

"What did you say your name was again?"

"Andromeda Hartley."

"You're the one who got the restaurant. You and your husband." The sweet tone now held an edge to it.

"It ain't right, because you ain't her family. Never will be. I don't have to tell you nothin'." The phone went dead in my ear. I set the phone down and looked at Ben.

"I heard." Ben shook his head. "Evidently the big Haggerty voice runs in the family."

"Oh, Ben. I sure hope this doesn't cause trouble for us. What if she contests the will because I called and upset her? I didn't mention anything about that, but still. . ."

"I don't think your call made her any angrier than she already was. And, if she does contest the will, it's not like she has a big case. She admitted she hadn't talked to Honey in almost ten years, even though she'd show up at the restaurant plenty enough."

"Wait!" I smacked the table. "I know who I can talk to—Esther. Do you think she'd know something? She's older than Honey by almost twenty years, but she's been around Greenburg forever."

"It's worth a shot." The phone rang on the table between us, and Ben picked it up. He spoke for a few moments, mostly monosyllables like, "Yes, no, okay. Oh. That's bad. Go on home." He ended the call. "Jonas has a family emergency. I need to go."

"Is Esther working tonight? Because if she is, I want to tag along and talk to her."

"She's there. She's training one of the newer waitresses, and I asked her to help keep an eye on the dining room. I think she'd make a great assistant manager."

"You don't say."

"I need to change." Ben headed to our bedroom to

add to our pile of laundry.

"I think it's great you're training her," I called down the hallway. "Does this mean she gets a raise?"

"Yup. I know she's used to getting tips, but maybe having a raise will offset that." He emerged from our room with a fresh T-shirt on. "I'm thinking of getting matching polo shirts for all the staff to wear."

"Nice."

"But I don't want to act too quickly. If anything happens and they contest Honey's will. . ."

"Don't think about that. We'll have to pray about that whole situation. Plus, if Gabe Davis is innocent, wherever he is, I hope you'll give him his job back."

Ben took me into his embrace once more before we left for the restaurant.

Esther sat across from me in the storage room/pantry of Honey's Place. We lounged on metal folding chairs in the makeshift break room. She kicked off her loafers and started rubbing one of her feet.

"You don't mind, do you?" Esther worked on her big toe joint. "Twelve hours on these old bunions is a killer."

"Um, go right ahead." I sipped my diet soda, reminding myself I needed to go back to Shapers. After all, I was paying for a monthly membership and I'd been only once in the past two weeks. "I wanted to talk to you about Honey. You knew her a long time. She and my aunt were friends, and I'm looking for someone they both knew. Bobby Johnson."

"Oh, you're right. I knew Honey way back. Still remember years ago when she went off one weekend to Bossier City, Louisiana. Won big at the casinos. I don't know how much, but wow. She won enough to buy this land and building and turn it into a restaurant." Esther shook her head. "She hired me when my husband died, was always very good to me. I've been here about twenty-eight years. And I'm still here after she's gone. Either you loved her or hated her, but nobody felt much in between about Honey. Man, I need a cigarette. You got any more questions?"

"Do you remember my aunt or Bobby Johnson?" She hadn't really answered my question before.

Esther nodded. "Crazy in love. Knew they were bound to run off at some point. Guess they did, right before Honey struck it big in Bossier. I don't know if they did for sure, and Honey never said if she knew. One day they were just gone and no one ever saw them again."

"Thanks for your help. I appreciate it." I watched her slide her cushioned shoe back on.

Esther touched my shoulder before leaving the storage room. "Not a problem. I know you're tryin' to find out about your aunt. I hope you find what you're lookin' for."

So did I.

When I entered the kitchen, I glimpsed someone with a head of red hair in the dining room. The sight made me pause.

"I know," said Ben. He stood at the order board. "She looks a lot like Honey, doesn't she?"

"Gretchen Wilkes." I couldn't keep from staring, just like a driver passing by a wreck on the highway. Looking at the woman from a distance, it was hard to tell which sister was older. "Are you going to introduce yourself?"

"I don't know." Ben looked thoughtful. "It used to drive Honey crazy, just seeing Gretchen sitting in a booth and eating lunch. Honey told us once that Gretchen probably buys her hair color from the same beauty supply store that Honey does. Or did."

Gretchen kept flipping through the menu. She placed it on the table in front of her. Then she studied the walls. One wall, the one behind the cash register, had autographed photos of different celebrities who'd stopped at Honey's Place. Gretchen pulled a notepad from her purse and started writing. She squinted at the ceiling and the lamps that hung over each booth and the ceiling fans that hung above the center of the room. I had to admit the pressed tin ceiling was a classy touch.

"Ben, I hate to say this, but it looks like she's casing the place. Or at least appraising it." I frowned. "I need to find out what she's doing here. If she sees you come from the kitchen, she'll know it's you. Or know you work here. And that I'm with you."

"What good will it do to find out why she's here? We already know that Honey left her out of the will because of their strained relationship." Now Gretchen was flagging down a waitress. She pointed at the menu.

"Because I want to know. If there's a threat to our livelihood, I want to see it coming. I'm not going to ignore it or pretend it won't happen." Gretchen started to turn to look into the kitchen, so I ducked behind the warming racks around the corner.

"I'm not pretending there's not a problem." Ben moved to the order board, where slips of paper from the order pads hung. "She can contest the will all she wants. But it'll take a judge to decide if she has any grounds to lay claim to the restaurant."

"And all it takes is a sympathetic judge to believe that a blood relation has more rights to this place than whoever Honey chooses. Do you want to share the restaurant with her, or worse, lose it altogether?" I dared not look around the corner again.

"There's no arguing with you, and I'm not about to start." A flare-up at the grill caused Ben to dart in that direction and grab a spatula. "But if she starts getting suspicious, just go ahead and leave. I don't want to stir up more problems if she thinks we're spying on her."

"She's spying on us. I mean you."

"I have nothing to hide, darlin'."

"Well, I'm going out the back door and come back around the front. There's a dirty booth across from her table. Can you get Esther to clean it off? I'll sit there. And whoever's station I'm in? Tell them not to let on they know who I am." I joined him by the grill. "Love you. And now I'll be out of your hair."

"Just don't start any trouble." He went on to coordinate the culinary dance in the kitchen without me.

I left through the back door of the restaurant, pinching my nose at the odor wafting from the Dumpster. The large metal box gave me a flashback to last summer, when I was arrested for Dumpster-diving and attempted stealing from a Dumpster. But I didn't take anything, and just Dumpster-diving by itself isn't a crime.

Slow down. My heart hammered in my chest. I wished Ben understood I was doing this for him. If Gretchen had plans, then I wanted to know about them. Forewarned and forearmed. Not that we could stop her.

Sweat beaded on my forehead. I felt as if I'd run laps around the parking lot as I pulled open the glass front door and entered. That booth had better be cleaned off. I couldn't very well sit at a dirty table if there happened to be a clean one nearby.

Esther was an angel. A set of fresh napkins with silverware rolled up inside each of them graced the table. No one else seemed to notice my entry as anything other than one more dinnertime customer. Perfect.

I sat down and fanned myself with the menu. "Phew. Humid out there."

Gretchen nodded across the aisle. "You got that right." Truly, the woman had the soft drawl of a Southern lady. Yet I'd heard the Haggerty shriek through the phone earlier that night.

One of the newer waitresses, Trina, took my drink order and removed the extra silverware from the table. "Thanks. I'll be eating alone tonight." She gave me a quizzical look and headed to the kitchen.

The lights clicked on in the parking lot outside. I watched dusk fall and contemplated what to say next. I fiddled with my napkin. Trina returned with my iced tea.

"Thanks." I smiled up at her.

"You ready to order?"

"Um, just a few more minutes. I can't decide." This was true enough. I'd planned on going to Shapers for a workout and instead ended up having a second dinner at the restaurant. I'd make up for missing my workout in the morning. I debated between ordering the taco salad or the grilled chicken.

"Okay. I'll be right back." Trina moved on to another table.

I unrolled my silverware and looked at the fork. Yuck. Something made it through the dishwasher that shouldn't have. I ought to mention that to Ben.

"Need another set of silverware?" Gretchen held a rolled-up bundle across the aisle.

"Oh, yes, thank you. I've got something on my fork." I frowned. "I've never had this happen before, not here, anyway."

"Do you come here often?" Gretchen folded her notebook shut. I tried not to look wistfully at the pad of paper as she slid it into her purse.

"Oh, a few times a week." True enough. "Honey's has the best pies in town. Or had, I should say. I found them hard to resist, so I never looked at the dessert menu if I could help it."

Gretchen blinked hard a few times, then dabbed at her eyes with a napkin. "Yes, the best pies." Then she smoothed over her expression. "Sorry about that."

"Are you okay?"

"I. . .my sister passed away."

"Were you close?"

"No. Not really. And she left me nothing. Times are tough." Gretchen shrugged. "But you've got to take care of family, no matter the bad blood between you. I thought she would have realized that."

"I really am sorry." Now what would I do? This woman had no clue I was Andi Hartley. Her demeanor would certainly be different if she did.

"Don't be sorry. She was aimin' at trouble for years, and she sure found it." A clatter in the kitchen made us both look in that direction. "I smell a rat, and I don't mean the kind with a tail."

"Huh?"

"She left what was rightfully mine to someone else. Someone not even family. And she'd told me she would remember me when she passed away. I thought for once I'd be taken care of." Just then, Trina approached with Gretchen's order. House special, the Bongo burger— Ben's original recipe. Honey had incorporated it into her latest menu change.

"You ready to order?" Trina stopped at my table.

"Taco salad." I smiled at her.

"I'll put that in for you." When Trina left, I glanced at Gretchen, who had just taken her first bite of burger. She rolled her eyes and chewed.

"Umm. . ." Gretchen glanced my way. "I haven't had a burger this good in ages."

I wanted to remark that I'd had one last night at home, same recipe. Then a thought broke over me like a wave of ice water. What if Gretchen had assumed Honey would leave her the restaurant? What if in her dire financial straits she'd murdered her own sister and waited to cash in? I'd seen one sister kill the other last summer. Jealousy and passion. What if the same thing had happened here? I knew I needed to fill Jerry in on this. That is, if he hadn't questioned Gretchen already. Jerry's lips couldn't be pried apart with a crowbar, especially with those photographs coming out and Ben on the suspect list.

The next time Trina passed my table, I stopped her. "Could I have my taco salad to go?"

❦

True to my earlier resolve, I went to Shapers the next morning before heading to the store. I needed to think, and what better way than to crank up the MP3 player and hit the treadmill.

My legs burned, but I didn't care. My mind burned, too. I could pencil a chronology in my head from the time Aunt Jewel left town to the time I followed Spot out into our muddy watermelon field. Nothing told me who would have a motive to kill Aunt Jewel, or why. Then I thought about the new information that arose last night about Gretchen Wilkes. She definitely had a motive for killing Honey. At least I thought so. The two cases competed for my attention.

Vivian emerged from the office. Her makeup-free eyes didn't look like cats' eyes this morning. Instead she wore simple narrow-framed glasses. She moved to the kick-boxing bag dangling in the far corner of the mirrored room and started going at the bag like it was her worst enemy.

I wondered what had happened. After Honey's death and my realization that I'd blown chances to get to know a lonely soul, I'd prayed during my quiet times for chances to reach out to people and be a friend. In our rat-race world with its crazy schedules, sometimes we let people slide by too often.

Should I spend ten more minutes on the treadmill or stop now and talk to Vivian? I decided to wait instead of accidentally being on the receiving end of a roundhouse kick from one of her wiry yet muscular legs. *She must burn a ton of calories.*

Ben had come home late last night, but I didn't find myself frustrated or pensive. Not only did I chat with Esther and find out a little more about Honey, but I saw firsthand Ben's talent in the kitchen. And I saw how the other employees respected him. He wasn't zany like Honey. Yet they followed his lead and the dinner crowd flowed in and out all evening.

He'd found his passion, or so it seemed. I thanked God and Honey for helping him. Part of his reason for leaving long-haul trucking was me. That much I knew. He'd decided he was ready to settle down. But settling down didn't mean a rut. I hoped he wasn't headed for one at the restaurant. I know I couldn't bear living in a state of sameness all the time. Trouble is, whenever I felt that strangulation, I tended to get antsy. I couldn't help it. And then Ben would dig in his heels. I didn't want to say the honeymoon was over, though.

Falling in love was the easy part. But staying in love required work, commitment, and overlooking lots of faults on both sides.

I glanced up. Vivian had quit attacking the bag and moved instead to a mat where she stretched. Splits. I could never do those. With a quick flick of my finger, the pace increased. Jogging. That I could handle. If I did enough time on this thing, I'd work off the extra biscuit from the other night at Momma's, or the half-slice of chocolate applesauce cake.

Momma still hadn't decided what to do about a memorial service for Aunt Jewel. Now that her remains had been released by the authorities, Warner's Chapel of Peace told Momma to take her time.

By now my legs screamed for mercy, and I figured I'd had enough cardio. Vivian chose at that moment to emerge from her concentrated stretching. We met at the water cooler.

"I feel so invigorated." Vivian took a sip of water from a paper cone. "Almost human again. What a day."

"Having a bad one already? It's sort of early for that." I got my own cone of water. Hopefully the thing wouldn't spring a leak.

"Feelings leftover from a really lousy yesterday. Actually, the past few weeks. Okay. This year." Vivian made a face at herself in one of the mirrors. "Ever since we came to Greenburg."

"What's wrong? That is, if you want to talk about it."

"I. . .I don't really have anyone to talk to around here." She leaned against the counter. "I. . .I think Curtis is seeing someone else. At first I only had suspicions, but one night I followed him. I confronted him about it, and he said he'd never see her again. He promised me."

"Who. . .never mind." I didn't need to know, and now because of one little word, she would probably tell me.

"I never knew. But he had that guilty look. He was sweating like a pig in August. Oh, wait. It is August. Anyway. . ." Her face paled. "I'm afraid I'm going to lose him. I thought with us moving to a small town, we'd slow down, spend more time together. Before we moved here, he met a woman online at a fan site for that actor Brent Balducci. Of course it's uncanny how he looks like the guy, so she was almost stalking him. But Curtis promised me they were just friends. Now I guess he's found someone else to spend time with. In person."

This was one time I thanked God those photos of Ben weren't the whole story, or the whole truth. "Oh, Vivian. I'm sorry."

"I can't sleep. And if I don't do something to keep him interested, I'm afraid he'll leave." Good thing she didn't put mascara on that morning. With her tears, she'd get a raccoon look. My heart went out to her.

"I'm just a newlywed. But I still know that relationships are work." Great, a platitude, just what Vivian needed. "Try loving him the way God loves him." I hoped that didn't sound like sermonizing.

"I'm not very religious. At all." She crossed her arms in front of her.

"What I mean is, look at his heart, and see *him*. One thing that happens to Ben and me is we get so busy. Same house, separate vehicles, separate lives almost. Sometimes I see his laundry more than him. And something happened the other day that scared me."

"Which was?"

"A glimpse of what life would be like if he *weren't* true to me and I couldn't trust him." I took another sip of water. "But I realized I can trust him and do, and I never stopped. As long as we keep looking at each other's hearts like God does, we'll stay close. Or at least not very far away."

"That's nice if it works for you." Vivian moved behind the counter and scanned the calendar. "Curtis gets so angry sometimes. . ."

"Really? He always seems so laid-back."

"He puts on a good public face. He doesn't hit me or anything. He gets in these blue moods, making me feel like I'm trying to measure up to an unspoken standard. He's impossible to please."

"Do you ever just talk to him like this?"

She shook her head. "And I'm afraid if I try to 'see him,' like you say I should, he won't let me. Some mornings, like today, he shuts me out."

The door to the gym opened, and a pair of exercisers entered. Vivian turned to greet them with her best smile. She glowed from her workout, and neither of the other women probably guessed she'd been dabbing at her tears a scant few minutes before.

I went for my gym bag and gave Vivian a half-wave before heading to the locker room. My personal troubles seemed smaller, especially thinking of Ben.

Once I arrived at Tennessee River Soaps, I straightened my displays and downloaded a list of Internet orders for Sadie to fill and package on her next scheduled work shift. Then I called Jerry to tell him my suspicions about Gretchen Wilkes. Maybe he had already checked her out, but she might have fooled him with that sweet exterior she put on when she wanted to. She'd shown me that quick-change act at the restaurant with the emotion she'd shown about her sister. But her resentment toward Ben and me over the will showed her sweetness didn't run too deep.

Fortunately, I caught Jerry at his desk. "Good, you're there."

"Fleta said you had some news for me." Fleta, the ever-efficient bailiff, dispatcher, and sometime receptionist, had put me "right through" as she put it, only after quizzing me about the details of my call, which I managed to keep as vague as possible.

"Yes, I do. I had an interesting conversation with Gretchen Wilkes last evening. Did you know that she really resented Honey changing her will? If there's a chance she knew about this ahead of time, she might have killed her."

"Or more logically, she might have tried to butter up her sister in an attempt to get back in her good graces. If Gretchen had killed Honey, she definitely would not have done it before she'd gotten that will changed to benefit her." Jerry's tone made me feel like a child. "Why kill her? Why not just get Honey to change her mind?"

"Oh. I didn't think of that. But what if Gretchen tried to do that the other night, and Honey wouldn't budge? What if Gretchen lost it? Judging from the way she screeched at us over the phone the other night, she has a temper to match her sister's." I clicked onto my Web site. Maybe it was time for an update. I'd have to check the store's budget and see if I could afford that.

"How did you gain this new information, if she 'screeched' at you over the phone the other night?"

"Last night she showed up at Honey's Place, with a notebook in hand." My heart pounded at the recollection of Gretchen assessing the restaurant as if she were an interior designer planning a renovation. "So, I had dinner next to her booth. Struck up a conversation."

"She didn't know who you were?"

"I'd only talked to her once over the phone, and that was just for a few minutes. Anyway, she told me that Honey had left what was rightfully hers to someone else who wasn't family. She also said Honey had promised to remember her when she passed away."

"That doesn't mean Gretchen killed her."

"Jerry, you're supposed to be helping us here. Ben is a suspect. I'm just asking if you've included Gretchen in your investigation."

"Calm down. Ben is my brother. I'm giving the

DA all the information related to the investigation. Including Gretchen and other people in Honey's circle."

"I'm sorry. I was thinking of Ben, too. He didn't seem too worried about Gretchen, though." I fell silent. I didn't want to talk too much to Jerry about Ben's involvement in the case. That way if the DA or anyone else asked Jerry, he couldn't share what I didn't tell him. "But we did consult with Honey's lawyer about the restaurant, and we secured Drew Michaels for Ben."

"I'm glad you did that. Because if I need to speak with him again about the night Honey died, Drew will be there."

"That's right."

"Good." Jerry paused. "Andi, I know this is hard for you, but hang in there. There have been some developments in the case, and I hope to have some news for you soon. Very soon."

We ended the call, and I spent the rest of the morning and early afternoon waiting on customers. When I had a lull, I rested my feet in my small office nook.

Why did the situation with Gretchen bother me so much? Besides the fact that suspicion had been thrown onto Ben and I wanted his name cleared, of course. Lately I'd spent time resenting the restaurant, or at least Ben's commitment to his job and his employer. My expectations of what married life was supposed to be like had fallen short.

The idea of us possibly not having the responsibility of the restaurant should have relieved me of the burden.

But then what would we do for income? We still had meager savings, but we couldn't live on that and what Tennessee River Soaps made every month. And with Ben as a suspect, if he were actually charged with the crime, it wouldn't surprise me if Gretchen got her way and Honey's Place went to her.

Worrywart. I'd spent more time fussing and running around trying to fix things, when I hadn't prayed about Gretchen at all. I had to admit to myself that if a friend had come to me, I'd have encouraged her to pray. I sighed and reached for the phone. Taking my own advice would be a start. I decided to call Ben and see if he could sneak out and bring us lunch.

Thirty minutes later, Ben showed up with his newest menu item, a chicken strip tortilla wrap that made my mouth water.

"I came up with the recipe myself. It's lighter. At least it has low-fat salad dressing." He bit into his burger.

"Ben, I owe you an apology." I tried the tortilla wrap. If this was lighter, I'd eat this for lunch every day.

"What for?"

"For being so cranky. Being married is an adjustment. Doesn't it say somewhere that getting married is one of those 'big' lifetime events that can cause good stress? And another one is moving. And then there were two deaths, which means really, really bad stress."

"What are you chatterin' about?" He took his finger and oh-so-gently wiped a spot of salad dressing from my cheek. After my workout earlier that morning, by the time lunch rolled around I was ready to eat anything not nailed down. The soap had even started smelling delicious.

"We've had some life changes, and it's no wonder things have been crazy." My heart swelled as I looked at him. "But no matter what we go through, I wouldn't want to go through it with anyone else. I realized I ought to pray more and worry less."

"Same here. Except I don't think you need to ask my forgiveness. I haven't been easy to live with, in and out of the house all the time. Gone more than I'm home. And I missed your big night at the Chamber. I still feel rotten about that."

"Don't worry about it. Part of me realizes how much you love the restaurant, and you're committed to it." I waved off his words. "I just don't ever want to get so busy that you slip right by me. Or vice versa."

"I can promise you and God that ain't gonna happen." He leaned in for a kiss, which I gladly returned.

Then I took Ben's hand. "And I'm sorry, too, about freaking out like I did about the whole situation with Gretchen. I didn't mean you were ignoring it. I just figure we ought to pray about it. I feel a little sorry for her, being cut off from her sister like that, then losing her. It did bother me, though, the way she was looking at the place. As if she has plans for it."

Ben opened his mouth just as the phone rang.

The caller ID said Greenburg PD, so I snatched up the phone right away.

"I have some news. The news I was promising you before, in fact," Jerry said. "I tried calling Ben, but I was told he snuck out to your store, Andi."

"Yes, we're both here having lunch. I'm going to put you on speaker phone."

"All righty." His voice filled the room. "I wanted to let y'all know that we have a warrant out for the arrest of Gabe Davis for the murder of Honey Haggerty. We had an anonymous tip that placed him at the scene of the crime. That, and his wife told us he'd admitted to stopping by the restaurant the night Honey was murdered. Plus, you and a roomful of other people witnessed Gabe threaten her. To top it off, we found some physical evidence that he'd been involved in the struggle. Skin cells under Honey's fingernails. Someone spotted his truck in Selmer, so it's only a matter of time before we locate him and bring him in."

Ben and I stared at each other. I found my voice first. "Thanks for letting us know."

"Not a problem. Ben, I'll call you later." Jerry hung up.

"Gabe Davis, a murderer." I shook my head. "And he has so much to lose. His wife adores him, his little girl is a doll. Murder doesn't make sense. I mean, it never makes sense, but there's such a thing as self-control. He should have thought of his wife. His child."

With a rustle of paper, Ben folded up his empty burger wrapper and tossed it in the trash. He began striding around the small sales floor. "It doesn't feel right. Honey fired him, but I don't think Gabe would have killed her. I really don't. I betcha Jerry has the wrong guy."

"What can we do?" I watched him pick up a package of glycerin soap and sniff it.

"Only one thing to do. We've got to find the real killer. " He returned to the stool next to mine.

I nodded. "Maybe when the killer hears someone else was arrested, they'll relax. I still wouldn't be surprised if Gretchen had something to do with her sister's death."

"What about your aunt's case? Are you going to try to solve both of them?" Ben frowned. "I don't see how you'll have time to work on both."

"Whichever I pursue, I have a feeling I'll find the other killer, too." More was at stake than a hometown restaurant. I knew that God would take care of us, whatever happened to Honey's Place. But the fact that two people had been murdered, two one-time friends... I had to find the connection.

12

People usually heard Junker Joe Toms coming before they saw him. At Honey's small graveside service, he'd shown up thirty minutes late, his rust bucket of a truck chugging and snorting and spewing a smoky cloud from the tailpipe. Joe's truck looked bad and ran worse, and it was a wonder the vehicle ever passed inspection.

At the funeral, he'd been well-lubricated with his favorite brew and said nothing to us. Today he was the next stop in my search for Bobby Johnson. Joe and Honey had a curious relationship, and I never understood why they didn't just get married.

I pulled my Jeep up to Joe's storefront, which was actually the front of his house on a quiet side street near downtown. It looked like a perpetual yard sale. If you weren't careful, you might get lost in the maze of yard ornaments and old farm equipment. Somehow he'd gotten his property zoned commercial, and as long as he kept price tags on the stuff, nobody could complain about his yard. That, and no one wanted to see a flash of Honey's wrath if they complained.

A handpainted sign, JJ's JUNK, didn't seem necessary. The place was self-explanatory. I approached the chainlink gate to the front yard, realizing in all my years of growing up in Greenburg, I'd never crossed the threshold of Junker Joe's.

The hinges complained as I entered the yard.

Somewhere inside, a dog barked. Guitar music filtered to the screened-in front porch. The front windows were open, and a box fan roared in one of the openings that happened to lack a screen. I placed one foot on the front step. The guitar music stopped.

"About time you came by," a crusty voice said from inside the house. "C'mon in and get a sodie."

I entered the porch where Junker Joe had a desk set up and shelves along every wall. Wherever there wasn't a window, the shelves stretched to the ceiling. "Hi, Mr. Toms."

"Go ahead and call me Joe. I don't mind none." Joe came onto the porch. He wore the same plaid shirt he'd had on the day of the funeral. Once I really looked at him, I realized he was no more than fifteen years older than I was. Years of hard living had etched a map across his face, noticeable despite the shadow of beard. That was unusual. He'd shaved his customary hairy face for Honey's funeral. I imagine she'd have flipped if she knew. On more than one occasion I'd seen her tug on his beard before giving him a quick kiss on the cheek. Now it looked like Junker Joe was trying to get the beard back.

"Okay, Joe." I glanced at a shelf. Did I need an old waffle iron? Still in its original box, a bargain at five bucks. A film of dust on the cover begged me to run a finger across the surface. Momma would be running around with a dust rag and throwing all the boxes and old magazines in the trash. "So, how are you doing since. . ."

"Been holding up." He gave a solemn nod. "It ain't

the same without her around here. Too quiet. I ain't had a good shoutin' match in too long."

"It definitely hasn't been the same. We've been scrambling at the restaurant. Or, I should say, Ben has."

"I told Honey she was full of stale pork rinds, willing that whole thing to y'all. Your man don't have the experience for running a place like that. No offense."

"None taken. I was totally surprised when the lawyer read her will." A potential sneeze tickled my nose. "Owning a restaurant sure wasn't in our plans. If it's any consolation, I'm waiting for the other shoe to drop to see if her sister contests the will. But as far as I know they haven't spoken in years." I regretted the words as soon as they came out. Who knew if Joe would run and say anything to Honey's family?

"You know, Honey was closer to me than to her own family. I been around her longer than you and your truck-driver cook."

I shivered. "You're right. I agree. You were closer to her. You knew her better than anyone, probably. And that's why I came. I'm trying to find Bobby Johnson. He and my aunt—"

"I know. They ran around with Honey. We all did. No more than kids, really, who thought they knew everything." Joe rubbed his chin. "And Honey thought the world of your family. Didn't want to cause you pain."

"Ironic." I found a chair covered with stacks of *Popular Mechanic* magazines on sale, twelve for three dollars, stacked the magazines on a nearby box, and took the seat I'd cleared for myself. "With her will, she left a note for us. She mentioned making up for what she'd done. Do you know what she was talking about?"

Joe nodded. "It's time for me to show you what Honey left for you." He shifted to stand, joints popping for one so relatively young. "Be right back. Get you a sodie from out o' the cooler."

Joe disappeared into the main part of the house, and I spied a cooler next to his desk. I found a can of diet cola floating among other cans in the melting ice.

A fly buzzed at the top of one of the windows. I watched it struggle against the glass. The outside and freedom lay beyond the pane, just like my answers lay at the other side of what I could see. *Just give me a bread crumb for a few more steps on this trail.*

"Here we go." Joe reemerged from his house. "Honey gave this to me a long, long time ago. She knew nobody would find it here, and she trusted me with it." He handed me a vinyl suitcase, a shiny light beige that had once been white, covered with large neon flowers. "People want to protect the ones they love. She didn't want any questions popping up. Even if someone found the suitcase way back when, oh. . . what a mess for a lot of people. That and your papaw, full of fire 'n' brimstone and all of God's wrath."

I placed the soda on a nearby shelf and checked the suitcase's tag. But I didn't need to. Once upon a time, I'd seen its cousin, a larger suitcase, in my grandparents' closet. "Aunt Jewel's. When did Honey give this to you?"

"Almost thirty years ago."

"Honey knew Aunt Jewel was leaving." I sank back

onto the empty chair. "All those years."

Joe took his place behind his desk. He might have worn a tailored suit, the way he situated himself in his chair. "I wasn't goin' to say anythin', and she made me promise not to. I shoulda married her when she asked. Maybe none of this would have ever happened."

"What? *She* asked you to marry *her*?"

"Impossible to wrap your mind around that one? Believe me, I know." He shrugged then grabbed a flyswatter. He leapt to his feet and whacked the pesky fly in the window. "Take that, ya booger!"

His sudden action made me jump. "But you didn't get married."

"No. She changed her mind after Jewel disappeared. Wouldn't tell me where she got the suitcase, either. I wonder if anyone else knew about it. . ."

"And killed Honey for it?" I set the suitcase down as if germs coated it. They probably did, and I didn't care to think about that. "But why? Who would kill Honey because of a suitcase? Especially if it's been here for thirty years. I'm trying to find Bobby Johnson. I bet he'd know."

"Bobby left when Honey went away and won big at the casinos. Same weekend. You remember times like that." Joe sighed and reached for a cigarette and lighter and tugged an empty coffee can toward him. I couldn't stand the smell of cigarette smoke, but on the other hand, I couldn't leave without hearing everything Joe had to say. "Honey came back, guns blazin', but Bobby didn't. We thought Jewel left with him."

"We all did. Joe, I already know about Jewel not

leaving. She's been in the watermelon field for years. But what is it I don't know?"

"Just take the case and go. I didn't want anyone to find out about it and come after me." Joe blew a smoke ring then waved as if to send me off.

"Thanks for telling me about this." *I think.* "I'm going to turn the suitcase over to the police." Time to leave the smoke-filled junk room. But I didn't agree with Joe. Now that Jewel's body had been found, the fact that she hadn't left made the suitcase a nonissue. At least it was to me. No one would be coming after Joe.

"They got the wrong guy, you know." Joe's words made me stop my trek to the door. "I don't want to say anythin' much since you're rubbin' shoulders with that crowd. But Roland and Honey. . ."

"I know about them. But I understood that was a long time ago."

"You don't know about her ads in the paper, do you?"

"What ads?"

"It had to do with money. Had to. The green stuff really turned Honey into a wildcat. If she could get it, she would. Spent it, too. That customized Harley of hers wasn't cheap." A gleam entered his eye, which gave me a thought.

If the will said anything about her Harley coming to us (which I definitely didn't want, and Ben had better not want, either), and no one contested the will, I'd talk to Ben about giving the motorcycle to Joe. Ben wasn't into motorcycles, anyway. At least I didn't think so. Or he'd better not be.

Joe opened his mouth, and his phone shrilled.

Before he answered it, he looked at me. "Go. Now. I'm not telling you anythin' more."

Fine. All I wanted to do was leave. I knew I should take the suitcase directly to Jerry, but I wasn't going to just yet. I was going to Momma's instead. She and Diana and I needed to look at the contents. I wasn't about to do it without them. A finger of doubt niggled my mind, but I wasn't about to let Jerry be the first one to see some of the last things my dead aunt had ever touched.

"I'm so glad I have the afternoon off." Di sat across from me at Momma's kitchen table. "I would've been mad if you'd done this without me."

Chances were, the suitcase and its contents would vanish again, this time relegated to an evidence locker and not a junk store. I promised myself to be very careful as I examined its contents. Aunt Jewel had packed this little suitcase with hope, expectancy, and love. Had she sung a song in her heart as she made plans to start her life with Bobby? She loved him enough to at least consider leaving her whole life in Greenburg behind her.

"Well, get on with it then." Momma stood by the stove and looked at the suitcase as if it were a wild animal that had crawled up onto the table to attack her.

"Okay." I pulled on a pair of Momma's disposable stretchy gloves that she used when she touched up her roots. "I realize this could be evidence. But I want us to see it before turning it in to Jerry. Di, do you have the camera ready?"

Di waved the camera in front of me. "Got it."

The metal zipper glided easily around the edge of the suitcase. When I lifted the top, a musty smell drifted up. I didn't have to look at Momma to know she was crying. A lump swelled in my throat. Aunt Jewel had probably been the last person to zip this case closed. I fought to speak around the lump. "Okay, here's some clothes. She was so little. These are genuine vintage now. Rags Fifth Avenue downtown would sell these for big bucks. A cosmetic bag." The camera flashed.

Di leaned over the case. "Unzip the bag so I can get a good shot."

"Back up." I touched Di's shoulder. "Don't you watch CSI? Not completely realistic, I know, but you might contaminate this with stray hairs."

"As if it's not contaminated already."

Jerry was going to be angry that I hadn't brought the suitcase to his office straightaway. But I couldn't do that to Momma.

The cosmetic bag contained a bottle of perfume, a Cover Girl compact, remarkably still intact, some mascara, several tubes of lipstick, and a bottle of red-hot nail polish.

"I can smell her perfume." Momma clutched her throat. "Sweet Honesty. Avon." Then we found a simple white cotton dress with a longish skirt, something a young woman might wear to elope.

"We don't have to do this." I paused, clutching a lime green polyester blouse with one hand. Aunt Jewel had worn this blouse and loved it enough to want to take it with her.

"No. We need to see if there's a locket in there. Daddy had given it to her on her eighteenth birthday. I don't want anything else." Momma slipped from the kitchen and returned with a photo album. She ran her hands over the cover. "We took some pictures her last day with us. Didn't realize then it would be the last time we'd see her. But here's pictures of the locket."

Di and I hovered over the album and looked at the pictures. Jewel grinned as she held a velvet box open toward the camera. Inside was an elegant heart with a filigree swirl on the front.

"See the next picture? The locket opens into four sections. My momma had put pictures in there. For when Jewel went away to college one day." Momma looked lost in memories, so we let her talk. "No wedding for her to that good-fer-nothin', at least where our daddy was concerned. She was supposed to go to college and 'make something of herself.' "

"I meant to tell you, when I visited Papaw the other day and Jerry questioned him, Papaw said something about a locket. He. . .thought I was Jewel and demanded to know why I'd lost it. " Underneath the blouse, I found a pair of striped polyester pants with thirty-year-old creases. "Do you recall if there are any hidden pockets in the suitcase? Somewhere she might have hidden something valuable."

"I don't know. It's been years." Momma came closer as Di snapped a picture of the pants.

"Unless she was wearing the locket when. . ." I

wiped my forehead with my sleeve. "But then Jerry didn't say if they found a locket in the field."

"I sure hope it's in here." Momma looked hopeful. "Maybe Jerry would let me keep it if it's not vital to the investigation."

"Hang on, I think I've found something. Part of the lining is cut. There's something stuck inside." Even through the glove, I could feel paper. A flat bundle of—

"Twenty-dollar bills." I let the banded packet of bills fall onto the folded blouse.

Di's voice came out in a squeak. "That's got to be a thousand dollars. We band them like that at the bank."

"I think we're finished here." I looked at Momma and wiped the tears from my cheeks. "We need to call Jerry right now."

Jerry's face flamed. Other than that, he looked like he normally did. Although, when I looked closer, I saw that he'd styled his hair to tame his unruly curls. Had the man discovered hair gel? "Andromeda Hartley, you should have brought this to me right away." He reminded me of a giant teddy bear scolding and trying to look stern. "You could have jeopardized this entire case."

"I was careful. I used gloves. And everything's here. You know it's all going to sit in an evidence room somewhere until someone gets around to looking at it. Priorities and case loads and all that. You know that you are all overworked, underpaid, and the trail of Honey's killer is a lot fresher. I figured it wouldn't hurt if I tried checking things out myself, especially since y'all are busy with Honey's case." I glanced at the desk. Jerry had a chef salad instead of his usual double-decker brute burger. Strange.

"Jewel's case is an ongoing investigation. The DA doesn't care if it's thirty years old or not." Jerry paced his office, walked to the window overlooking the police station's back parking lot, and then turned to face me.

"I know that." I rubbed my forehead, and tears burned my eyes. "But just think of where that suitcase has been for thirty years. In a junk store, getting plenty contaminated. I didn't think too hard about what we were doing. Not at first." I sank onto an empty chair across from Jerry's desk. Trouble. I'd found it. I should have gone with my head instead of my heart, bypassed Momma's, and come straight here. "But please understand. I did it for Momma. That suitcase is the only link she has to her sister, and I wanted her to see it before it. . .before it disappeared or something."

"What am I supposed to do with you, Andi Hartley?" Another set of stalking steps brought Jerry back to his desk. His chair complained when he sat down. "Do you have so little confidence in us that we can't do our jobs?"

"I'm. . .I'm sorry. Really." My pulse pounded in my ears. I just knew my blood pressure had reached the top of Everest. "Am. . .am I going to end up in jail?"

Jerry sighed. "You could. Tamperin' with evidence.

Obstruction of justice."

"I didn't think—"

"You're right. You didn't think. Did you put the money back where you found it?"

I nodded. "If there's anything else in there, we don't know. We stopped looking after we found the money. But Aunt Jewel's locket is missing. She had just gotten it for a birthday present. Momma has pictures of it in her photo album at home. Do you remember if they found anything besides Aunt Jewel's remains in the field?"

"Besides some fabric, I don't recall that anything else was found." Jerry's face had now regained its normal color. "Actually, if they'd found anything of value, we'd have let you know. And we probably would have found a way to get it back to you if it wasn't vital to the investigation." He picked up the phone to call someone, presumably the evidence room. Or the county authorities. All I knew was I would likely never see that brightly colored case again.

"Jerry Hartley here. . . Yes, I have a new lead. I'm sending someone to talk to Joe Toms. . .right. Well, he'd better talk. I have some evidence in the Jewel Kincaid case I need to process. . .could be a break for us. But it may be contaminated." At Jerry's words, I cringed.

When he hung up the phone, I told him, "Thanks for what you're doing. I know you feel caught in the middle sometimes. And I'm sorry I did that to you. It. . .it wasn't fair." As brothers-in-law went, I had no complaints about Jerry. Other than the fact his approach to life was as laid-back as Ben's. Not that either of them was lazy, just that they didn't see the need to hurry about some things. Well, most things.

"I know you're sorry. But this puts me in a bad spot."

My brain floundered for a solution. "I want to give a statement. Maybe if they understand I wasn't trying to be reckless, and why I did what I did, that will help. Please?"

Jerry gave a slow nod. "I can't guarantee anything, but sure."

Twenty-five minutes later, I was done. Now I needed to pray for mercy and stay out of Jerry's way.

"Thank you, Jerry. And I promise, if I learn anything, I'll come to you right away."

"I'll hold you to that." Jerry reached for his salad. A good while ago, it probably had been fresh and crisp. Great. I'd ruined his lunch, too. "So, you ready for that festival?"

"Not hardly. I've been looking for Bobby Johnson and finding out everything else instead." I thought of the folder for the Watermelon Festival gathering dust on my desk. I also thought of Sadie's mushrooming paycheck as she covered the store for me while I gallivanted around. With her return to college looming, she wasn't complaining about the extra hours lately. "I'm hoping he'll turn up, somehow."

"Ben told me about those anonymous deposits in Honey's accounts. Thanks for the tip."

I still couldn't get over the sight of Jerry crunching on salad. "Ben found them in the records, so he gets the credit for it. But I'm hoping to find out who'd been paying her like that. I have my suspicions. Two men. Either Roland Thacker or Bobby Johnson."

"What's the reason she'd blackmail either one of them?"

I wanted to keep my promise to Roland not to let Cynthia know about what he'd done, but at the same time be truthful with Jerry. And then the long-ago affair might one day become public knowledge. "Secrets. Both men have them. Bobby might know what happened to Jewel, and if Honey needed the extra cash, she'd sell him her silence. And Roland. . .he couldn't stand her. She had dirt on him, too."

"Whatever you do," Jerry said around the mouthful of salad, "be careful. If you're right, and there's a murderer who's walked free for thirty years. . . Well, you know what they say about desperate times."

"I'll be careful. Like I said, I promise I won't get into any more trouble. Or cause any." And next I'd head to the newspaper office to see if they'd help me out.

Jerry's phone rang. He picked it up as I stood. "What's that? Great. I'll meet you there. Make double sure you do everything right. The DA wants this case closed down."

He ended the call and looked at me. "Gabe Davis has been apprehended, and we're bringing him in for the murder of Honey Haggerty. You should let Ben know he's off the hook."

13

The office of the *Greenburg Dispatch* buzzed with activity, as much as a small-town newspaper can. A harried receptionist pointed me to the classifieds desk. "You're just in time to make tomorrow's edition if you hurry," she said over the warbling phone.

"Need an ad?" asked the kid behind the desk. His streaked blond hair hung over one eye. Funny how the closer you get to forty, the more baby-faced someone looks who's closer to twenty. His expression told me he'd rather be anywhere else than behind a desk with mountains of paper and file folders.

"Actually, I was wondering if I could see some personal ads that a Harriet Haggerty ran in the past. Is that possible? Would you have that in your records? I imagine I could find copies of receipts in her office to confirm the ads, but I thought I'd ask you first."

When I said Harriet Haggerty, his expression grew more animated. "She's the lady who was murdered a couple weeks ago, isn't she? Did you know her?" He had the curious spark in his eye of a newshound. No doubt he wouldn't be long at the classifieds desk.

"Yes, and yes. My husband runs her restaurant. Or what used to be hers. We own it now. For the moment." I didn't want to think about the will. Still no news about any possible opposition from her family, but I sure wasn't about to share that with this kid. For all I knew, Gretchen Wilkes could be his great-aunt or something. Greenburg had unexpected branches of family trees. Long ones, too. At least Ben was in the clear now, and no threat of a murder charge lurked at our door. Or Gretchen's either, now that I thought about it.

The barely-out-of-braces young man at the classifieds desk grinned. If he turned out to be the son of someone I'd gone to school with years ago, I'd probably scream and run for a cane. "It's all computerized now. In fact, I helped set up the database last year while I was doing my senior journalism internship. Let me do a search under her last name."

A few lightning-quick keystrokes later, and he'd accessed all of Honey's ads. "Okay, looks like we ran ads once a week for six months. Same message, too. 'The hive is running low. Meet me at Patch, ten tonight. Bring nectar or feel the sting. Queen Bee.' Wow, sounds like a cryptic message. Any idea of what this could mean?"

I shrugged. "I'm not sure. But I'm going to try to find out. Could you print copies of those for me, please?"

"Not a problem." With another flash of a smile, he typed some more. "I'll be right back. The printer's in the other room."

Hive and queen bee. Honey, of course. Meet her at Patch. . .it sounded like a place. Watermelon patch, perhaps. Bring nectar? Obscure ads. Maybe it was a stretch for someone to consider that a blackmail message. Or maybe not. My brain hit overdrive. Had she meant to bring a payoff? I'd have to find out, and for my next idea, I'd need Ben's help.

The reporter returned from the printer. "Okay. Here's your copies."

"Thanks." I tucked them in my purse, and as I did so, I removed my wallet. "How much if I want to run the identical ad, say, for the next four weeks?"

The young man glanced from the computer screen to me. "Are you taking over as the queen bee?"

"Not exactly."

"Thirty bucks. I just need your information and payment."

I paused. What if whoever responded to these ads wondered who placed the new ones, talked to our friendly young man here, and then came after me? Or maybe they'd be afraid, wouldn't show up, and I'd be out thirty dollars. But I was willing to bet thirty dollars that curiosity would draw them to the field. So I gave the kid my name and address and paid him for the ad. After this my idea tank needed filling, because I didn't know what other leads to pursue. And true to my promise, I'd give copies of these ads to Jerry.

"Andromeda Hartley. . .since you and your husband own her restaurant now, are you trying to figure out what these ads mean?" With a grin like that, he should go into politics.

"Something like that." I slid my wallet back into my purse. "I have some questions I'd like answered."

"You sound like a detective," he observed. "I happened to take an investigative journalism course in college. We could team up. All kinds of people come through the office here, plus I could ask key individuals in town some questions."

"I sort of work alone. Anyway, the police have arrested someone for Honey's murder, so that's not really what I'm focusing on at the moment." Since this would be common knowledge soon, I saw no harm in mentioning it to the young man. It was like tossing him a bone to gnaw on while I ran the other way.

"Do you have any ideas, though, about what the ads meant? I wonder if these ads bothered someone enough that they murdered her." The boy leaned back in his chair and rubbed his chin. "You see the weekly pattern."

"Wow, are you sure you're not being wasted here at the classifieds desk?" I tried not to chuckle at his intensity.

"I'm only here part-time, filling in." He sat up straight again. "The key to being a great reporter is to keep your eyes and ears open for that life-changing story. And one day, I'm going to find it. That's what I ask myself every morning. Where's the story?"

"And with that drive of yours, I'm sure you'll succeed." I seized the opportunity to stand. "So, thanks for your help."

"Good luck with those ads. I hope you find your answers."

"Thanks." I smiled at him and turned to go. Somehow I suspected he'd be sniffing out leads on someone's story. A troubling thought told me he'd probably shadow me. I didn't like that. Worse, what if he caused trouble for Jerry's work on the case? Oh dear. I hoped I hadn't caused *more* trouble.

"Andi Clark—I mean Hartley, how are you?" I hadn't been paying attention to where I was going and almost plowed into Trudy from the coffee shop.

Today she wore a yellow straw hat with a red ribbon hanging over one shoulder. Her white peasant blouse and tan capris made her look extremely bohemian and definitely not something you saw every day in Greenburg. If I wore an outfit like that, I'd look really wrinkled, or have to spend too much time ironing. We Hartleys are strictly a wash 'n' wear household. Maybe it was all the ironing I did when I was growing up.

"Trudy. Hi. I'm doing great. Swamped, actually." Three of the vendors still hadn't paid the second half of their booth deposit, and my committee chairman gave me the job of playing phone tag, since I "didn't have to do much at that store." But I didn't tell Trudy this.

Trudy beamed. "Ready for the festival where we celebrate all that is watermelon? Can you believe it's this weekend already? I'm here checking on the Chamber's big ad. It's not like people in town don't know about the festival, but anyway, I'm head of publicity, and I don't want anyone thinking I'm shirking my job." All this she said without taking a breath, and she didn't turn blue, either.

"I've still got quite a bit to do this afternoon, but most of the vendors are confirmed and we have the out-of-town craftspeople arriving Thursday morning. We have setup on Thursday night, so I'll be at the festival grounds for that." I realized I missed Trudy's coffee and her chatter. Nothing like a mocha and good conversation.

"See ya then!" Trudy breezed off, and I hurried home. Hopefully Ben knew where the camcorder was. I had only a short amount of time before the Watermelon Festival sucked me into all its dark pink glory, studded with black seeds.

⁓

Saturday came, and what I really wanted to do was stay home and sleep. Greenburg's Watermelon Festival was in full swing. After spending all day Friday at the festival and most of Saturday morning (my faithful Sadie took over at the Tennessee River Soaps booth at three), I didn't care if I ever saw another watermelon again. Or its seeds. What had led me to say yes to emceeing the kids' seed-spitting contest? I spent the entire time holding a microphone and dodging both seeds and spit. The Chamber of Commerce newbie getting initiated. To make matters worse, those closest to me were sure to make some cracks about a future mommy in training. It was enough for me to run screaming to the Tennessee hills and hide in Papaw's old hunting shack.

"Are you sure this'll work?" I was so close to Ben inside our storage shed that I could smell his cologne. And he smelled mighty fine. Because we were going *out*. It was only back to the Watermelon Festival, but at least it was a chance for us to be together. He promised to win a bear for me at one of the watermelon-themed game booths. I think they called the game "Beary Watermelon," and it involved air rifles and watermelon-shaped targets.

Ben pushed the buttons on the digital camcorder. We'd used it on our honeymoon—a cruise along the Mexican Riviera and some sightseeing of Mayan ruins—and hadn't had time to use it since. Spot had been curious when Ben took out the camera and its attachments. Now she yowled loud enough so we could hear her in the shed, the big baby.

"It'll work. We've got a large enough memory card in there, and I've set the motion activation feature and the night filter. If anyone comes to that field, we'll catch them."

"Maybe this was a stupid idea." I frowned as Ben attached the camera to its adjustable tripod.

"But we're trying." Ben kissed me. "And that's not stupid."

"What did Jerry say when you told him about the ads?" I asked.

"He said they definitely sounded suspicious." Ben worked the controls on the camera.

"I just hope he doesn't send a car out here tonight or anything." I squinted through the cracks between the boards. "If someone does show up, I can just picture them driving off if they see anything out of place."

"Well, Jerry did say not to do anything heroic. And we'll be at the festival, anyway."

The wooden walls of the shed had cracks in them, but they weren't big enough to accommodate a camera lens. Ben drilled a hole through one of the knots and positioned the camera lens in front of the hole. He'd promised himself a new shed next spring, after this experiment in carpentry. I hoped it didn't rain tonight, because the roof leaked.

"Wait," I said. "With the camera in the shed, how's the motion sensor going to work?"

"Good point." Ben looked sheepish.

In the end, we rigged up what looked like a makeshift pile of junk next to the shed, which was actually our set of trash cans with scrap wood stacked on them, the whole thing covered with a tarp. Atop the heap we rested the camera. I draped plastic over the top of the camera, in case it rained.

Ben turned it on to check the display. "Perfect."

"So if someone comes here at ten, we'll catch them." I almost wanted to stay home and watch through the kitchen window, but the date with Ben meant more to me.

We left for the festival in the late afternoon heat, with promises of watermelon-flavored snow cones waiting for us at the festival. *Lord, thank You for this breather. Help us in our quest. I want to find out what happened. For Momma. For Jewel. For all of us.*

Once upon a time, the open field near the high school had grown cotton. This weekend we had transformed the grounds into a country fair paradise. Tears pricked my eyes. I used to poke fun at people who got involved in the community, as if they'd put on airs. But this was town pride, and a great show of it.

"I wish Honey could have seen this."

Ben tightened his grip on my hand as we negotiated the line of booths. "She would have been proud. She definitely liked to bring people together."

I saw Cynthia Thacker strolling the festival alone.

Her hair done, a casual pants suit in spite of the weather, she definitely remembered her place as an example of Greenburg "society." Recalling Roland's words the other day in his office, I hoped she loved her husband. And that he still loved her. Not that he merely didn't want his indiscretions uncovered. Our eyes met.

"Andromeda. Ben." She gave us the thinnest of smiles.

"Hi, Mrs. Thacker. Where's your husband tonight?"

"He's home. Couldn't make it tonight. It's a shame, really." Cynthia nodded to a passerby. "He's got a stomach bug, and he really wanted to be here. Doesn't want to let anyone down. People count on him to lead the way, especially as Chamber president."

"I hope he feels better soon."

Cynthia nodded then continued on her way without another word to us. I wondered if instead of making an appearance at the festival, Roland had decided to stay home and prepare to meet whoever took out Honey's ad. But Ben and I had already discussed the idea that Honey might have been blackmailing Roland. I tried forcing myself to relax and enjoy the atmosphere.

Kids darted back and forth between the booths. Some hollered for cotton candy. Squeals and screams came from the Tilt-A-Whirl and the Zipper. The festival planning committee had caved at someone's request to have a few carnival rides. Roland had coughed up the money for the rental at the last minute. A local bluegrass band had taken the stage, as had several other musical acts that were booked for the weekend.

Ben and I made a game of trying to see how many Chamber members we could spot at the festival, but it was hard with the swarms of people circulating around the grounds. Whoever spied the most members got to choose whichever ride they wanted to ride on, and the loser couldn't complain. I happened to know Ben would get seasick on the pirate ship that swung back and forth, touching the sky. Twilight came, and with it came more people, mostly packs of teens.

"Jerry's going to be busy tonight," Ben observed.

"I'm just glad I'm out with you." I smiled at him. He didn't look quite as tired as he used to. "Where are we on points? Did you see the Delanes yet, because I didn't."

He shook his head. "I have five points, and you have three."

"If I see Curtis and Vivian first, we'll be tied. I'm surprised they haven't come, as much as Vivian felt honored at joining the Chamber. And Curtis was supposed to sing a few songs at the bandstand. Evidently someone's playing up the fact that Curtis does a great Brent Balducci impersonation." If we didn't find them, Ben would make me go on the Tilt-A-Whirl. I got queasy just looking at that one. When I was seven, I made the mistake of going on the ride right after eating a big bowl of cheesy chili. I'll say no more.

Then I caught sight of Junker Joe, riding a bicycle along the midway and towing a small wheeled cart. He would stop at each trash can, study its contents, then move along. The time crawled toward nine.

Roland had stayed home. Maybe he actually *was*

sick, and I was just looking for someone to blame. Maybe tonight wasn't supposed to be about me hunting anyone, but having a night off and enjoying time with my husband.

"You're pretty quiet tonight." Ben slipped his arm around me. "You okay?"

"Just tired. And thinking." After we'd seen Cynthia, Ben had lived up to his promise and I now hugged a three-foot bear the color of oatmeal and wearing a baby blue bow. Still no sign of Curtis or Vivian Delane, though. Someone hollered near the bandstand about why wasn't Curtis there to sing tonight. Brent Balducci impersonation, indeed. I'd have to look the guy up on imdb.com sometime and see what the big deal was about the late middle-aged actor/singer.

A familiar-looking redhead wandered with two other women among the festival-goers. "Gretchen Wilkes. Straight ahead and coming this way." Ben glanced at me. "We can duck behind a booth so you don't blow your cover."

"No, that's all right." I smiled at him. "Gretchen seemed genuinely upset about Honey the other day, and she had no idea who I was. Sure, she was probably looking at the restaurant to see if it was worth fighting for. But I think sitting in that restaurant and seeing Honey's touches everywhere reminded her that she loved her sister, regardless of their past feuding. I was hoping to get the chance to talk to her sometime, to see if she might know who wanted Honey dead."

Gretchen drew closer and I caught her eye. She glanced from me to Ben, then back to me again. "I thought you looked familiar. Liked my sister's pies, did you?"

"I did. Andi Hartley." I stuck my hand out to shake hands with her, but she just stared at it like I'd tried to hand her a red-hot pan. "Everything I told you the other day was the truth. I liked your sister. She came on a little, um. . ."

"Strong?" Gretchen shifted from one foot to the other. "I grew up with her. Hard to get a word in edgewise most of the time, and when you did, you were wrong."

"I wanted to talk to you about Honey's death."

"The police already talked to me. They know she and I barely spoke the last ten years. Doesn't mean I'd kill her. We were kin, even though she didn't like to remember that."

"But can you think of anyone who'd want to kill her?"

"Don't you read the news?" She looked at me like I was a simpleton. "They arrested someone. A former employee." Here, she glared at Ben.

"I know. We don't believe they arrested the right person."

"It looks pretty cut-and-dried to me. She fired him and smeared his name, and so he wanted revenge. Sometimes people just. . .snap." At that, Gretchen snapped her manicured fingers.

"I don't think Gabe did it," I said. "He has a wife and a little girl. My husband's worked with him. He knows Gabe's a hard worker. He had two jobs. That's not a thief, or a murderer. Besides, Ben said Honey was giving him an advance on his paycheck, and he didn't steal anything."

Gretchen shook her head. "Y'all should be giving thanks it wasn't you, Mr. Benjamin Hartley, that was the one getting arrested. Seems to me you really liked Honey's pies, too, didn't you? They can get a bit messy, can't they?"

Ben and I looked at each other. *Nobody* called him *Benjamin*. And the crack about the pies could only mean. . .I had a flash memory of the photo of Honey, wiping pie off Ben's cheek.

"What are you talking about?" I clutched my giant bear a little more tightly.

"You had just as much a motive as that Gabe fellow." Gretchen pointed a finger at Ben. "Butter her up, charm her, get her to change her will. . .and then get rid of her."

"That's not true. I worked for Honey, and that was it."

"Pictures don't lie, do they, *Mrs.* Hartley?" With one more pointed look at both of us, Gretchen rejoined her friends and they headed off down the midway.

"We know now where those pictures came from." Ben watched them stop at a craft booth. "I'll have to tell Jerry. Not sure what's going to happen with that. She didn't ask for money or try to terrorize us. Maybe she wanted to throw doubt into your mind, and suspicion on me."

"I guess she figured since the police arrested Gabe, they're not looking at you anymore. Or her."

"What a tough cookie. She sure sympathized with you." Ben took the bear from my arms. "I think she hates men."

"Could be." I put my arm around him. "But I sure

love this man a lot."

"And I love you." His stomach growled. "I wouldn't mind getting somethin' to eat. The River Grille has steak wraps at their booth."

Two steak wraps later, we realized we needed to sit down in order to eat the giant tortillas stuffed with grilled steak strips, lettuce, tomato, and sour cream. Ben looked like a big kid with ribeye juice on his chin. "Let's go to my booth. We can sit and eat there. Then I can see how Sadie's doing. Maybe she was swamped today."

We headed in the direction of the display tent decorated with my vinyl TENNESSEE RIVER SOAPS banner. Sadie was wrapping someone's purchase. Her boyfriend sat in the corner of the tent and strummed his guitar.

"Mrs. Hartley, you made it back. I didn't think you were going to come back until closing." Her glance flicked to her boyfriend. Ah, young love.

"Ben and I decided to come and just have fun. Thought I'd stop by to see how you are." I moved around the display table and took an empty seat. Ben tucked the bear next to my feet.

"Tired. We've been busy, so I'm not complaining." Sadie flashed a smile at me. Then another for her boyfriend, who looked at her as if her words were music. They'd have a sad parting when Sadie left to go back to college in a couple of weeks.

"Y'all go ahead. The rides are still open and so are some of the games. Ben and I can handle things here for a while."

"Really? I was wantin' to go on the Ferris wheel. It's so romantic. But we'll come back and help you close up." With that, Sadie grabbed her purse. Her boyfriend took her hand, and they vanished into the milling crowd.

Ben settled onto the seat that Sadie's boyfriend had occupied. "They're good kids."

I took a bite of my steak wrap, chewed, and swallowed. "That they are. But it's bittersweet for me, watchin' them run around so in love. Aunt Jewel was Sadie's age when she died. So many hopes. So many years."

"Which is why maybe we'll get a few answers tonight."

"I hope so. No matter how people say to just let it go, let the authorities do their work, I can't." A woman from church, the new doctor, strolled past. Her olive complexion, ink black hair, and dark eyes made her stand out from the crowd. I could imagine her walking straight out of a sketch from *Aladdin*. But even if she were a close friend, I'd have a hard time telling her she looked like a beautiful cartoon character.

The doctor paused at our table. "Hello there. What kinds of soap do you have. . .besides watermelon?" Her voice sounded proper yet had a musical tone with the faintest touch of drawl.

"Hi, Dr. . . ."

"Mukherjee." She extended her hand, and we shook. Strong, confident grip with a small hand. "We go to the same church, don't we?"

I nodded. "I'm Andromeda Hartley, and this is my husband, Ben."

Her smile lit her face. "Okay. You're related to the police chief then."

"Guilty as charged." Ben wiped his hand on his jeans and shook hands with her. "So what do you practice? I'd heard Dr. Bradley added another partner to his clinic."

"I'm an OB-GYN." Dr. Mukherjee picked up a wrapped bar of Gardenia Frenzy and sniffed. "I love caring for future mothers. And I can barely keep back the tears every time I help bring a new life into the world. We're all miracles from God, ready to live out His purpose for us on this earth." She paused. "Sorry. I didn't mean to go on like that."

"It's all right." Her words ignited something in my heart. A child, a miracle from God. All I knew was now I wanted one. Scary, but I did. Sure, a little miracle might give her parents fits—I could see that with Di and her boys—but like a nurturing tigress, she wanted to guide them to be what God destined them to be. Maybe it was something that had built up in me over time and now poured out at Dr. Mukherjee's words. Maybe it was remembering that pregnancy test and how I wasn't sure what to feel when I saw the result.

"I love what I do, and I'm happy to be here." A shadow crossed her face. "Greenburg is so different from Atlanta."

"Well, here's a belated welcome to Greenburg. And to Greenburg Bible Church. I've seen you there, too, but we've been busy lately, so we haven't attended the midweek service this summer."

"Thank you for the welcome. And I understand about being busy." Dr. Mukherjee selected several bars of different scented soap. "I'll take these."

She paid for her soaps and went on her way. I sat down on my chair again. "That woman is a living doll. In another century she might have been a princess. Look how she carries herself. So elegant a book wouldn't budge on her head while she walked. You're right. Jerry has a crush on her."

Ben looked amused. "He hasn't mentioned anything to me."

"He's so dedicated to his job, I don't think he's thought about making the time to get to know someone. And you're right. He did race out the door when her car was getting towed the other day—he could have sent someone else. And Jerry had a *salad* for lunch the last time I saw him at the office. I meant to tell you that." My brother-in-law wasn't what you'd call fat, but he was a little, um, squishy. "Maybe he's trying to lose weight. I think they'd be cute together."

"My darlin' Ands, I think we just need to step back and stay out of the way. Stick to being a detective, not a matchmaker." Ben stood and took out his wallet. "I'm parched. You want a Coke, too?"

"Sure."

He moved toward the line of food booths across the way.

Jerry and the doctor. Talk about opposites. But she knew who he was. Maybe I ought to mention that to him. Except maybe she just had a memory for names and faces. A good doctor often did. So maybe I'd listen to Ben and not say anything to Jerry.

The rest of the night was a trickle of customers

as the festival wound down for the evening. Although Ben ended up winning our game, we never got to ride on the Tilt-A-Whirl. Sadie and her boyfriend returned to help us pack up. I'd decided not to keep my booth open on Sunday. After all, I closed on Sundays at the store. We loaded the rest of the soaps, tables and chairs, and display items onto Ben's truck and headed home.

I glanced at my watch with the aid of a street light. Eleven fifteen. "I wonder what the camera will show." We left the downtown neighborhoods behind us and crossed the bridge, moonlight flickering on the river below. Had the recorder done its job?

"We'll find out soon." Ben turned onto our road. "I'm just as curious as you are. Even wondered once or twice if our man was at the festival tonight."

"Me, too. I'd see a guy in his fifties and wonder if that was Bobby Johnson. He probably doesn't even live here anymore. I wondered who in the crowd might have secrets that Honey would blackmail for." We entered the driveway, and the watermelon field looked undisturbed, its large fruit giant lumps in the moonlight.

"Time to pick some more watermelon," Ben observed. "I wonder if we could set up a farm stand."

"I'm going to try Momma's recipe for pickled watermelon rind. Thought I'd can some."

"Is that so? Sounds mighty delicious to me."

Ben stopped the truck next to our awning, and we lost no time getting to the makeshift junk pile and our camera. He pushed some buttons and the display lit up. "Okay, it looks like something triggered the camera at nine forty-five."

My heart pounded. "What?" I looked closer at the LCD screen.

A deer strolled into view, hopping across the driveway and into the field. It froze as if it had heard a noise, then bounded away into the woods at the edge of the watermelon patch. Ben clicked on the fast-forward. Headlights skimmed across the screen. No one entered the driveway, but all vehicles passed by on the main road. Another deer. I couldn't tell if it was the same one from earlier. Eventually the memory card filled up.

"Nothing else." Ben turned the camera off.

"But at least the idea worked." I sighed. "We'll just have to try it again next Saturday night. Except this time I'm not going anywhere. I'm going to sit in the shed and watch until someone shows up."

14

On Monday I headed to Momma's to learn all about pickled watermelon rind. Now that the festival was over, all I had to do was run a business and find a murderer, so I figured my schedule had cleared. Sort of. I was fresh out of ideas in the sleuthing department, but maybe Momma would give me some helpful information.

She took a giant stockpot out of the refrigerator. "This pot is full of rinds and salt water. They've been soaking overnight."

"Are they chopped?" I looked inside the pot.

"Yes, but I only use the white part of the rind. I cube 'em, about one inch in size. Get me the other large pot and put water in it to boil." She drained the salted rind while I followed her directions.

Momma handed me her recipe card once the pot of water was on the stove. "Here's all the spices we need."

"I'll get 'em down from the cabinet." The simple act of cooking comforted me, more than a chunk of chocolate cake with fudge frosting. I could tell it meant something to Momma, too, spending time with her daughter in the kitchen. Vague memories flickered inside my head, of making cookies with her and trying to knead bread when I could barely see over the top of the counter.

Momma's shoulders slumped. "Jewel missed out on all o' this. She never got to have babies, see them grow up, and have their own. Never learned the treasure of family. Sorry. I didn't mean to add any sadness today. But I should tell you, I decided to have a memorial service for her a week from Thursday."

"Don't worry. You're not making me sad." I gave Momma a hug. "Aunt Jewel's been on my mind, too. She and Bobby Johnson."

Momma's mouth sealed into a thin line. Then she spoke again. "Here's the cheesecloth. Did you find the cinnamon sticks?"

"Yes. And the mustard seed and cloves."

She measured out the spices and wrapped them in a cheesecloth bundle. "Now we put this in another pot with vinegar and sugar."

"That's a lot of pots. Maybe when I make some pickled rind, I can get Ben to do the dishes." Momma had sure clammed up when I mentioned Bobby. "So, what was Bobby like?"

Her look could have pickled *me*. "Shaggy hair. That, I remember. Daddy always said he looked like a mangy dog, but Jewel thought his hair was 'groovy.' Not a big guy or a small fella. Medium, average. He'd sort of blend in most of the time."

"What do you think Aunt Jewel saw in him?"

"Watch the sugar and spices. Don't let 'em burn." Momma checked on the rinds and sighed. "What does any young woman see in a man? You know there's a verse in Proverbs about that, about four things too amazing to understand: 'the way of an eagle in the sky, the way of a snake on a rock, the way of a ship on the high seas, and the way of a man with a maiden.' Wish I understood. We'd have cured her of Bobby back then. Watch the stove. I want to show you somethin'."

Momma went into the living room and when she returned, she held a scrapbook, one I'd never seen before. Its pages held a set of newspaper clippings from the *Greenburg Dispatch*. "See. Here's what I've held onto all this time."

I nodded as I scanned the articles on the front page. Someone had spray-painted graffiti on the fountain in front of City Hall. Someone else complained at the county hearing about rising property taxes. A property developer wanted to add more stores at the edge of town. The main headline was a bank robbery over in Selmer the Saturday before. And someone else clamored for money to build a new gymnasium.

"It's a newspaper from the seventies."

"This is the first paper that came out after Jewel disappeared. Not a word about her. Nothing. Don't know why I kept the paper, but I did." Momma took the paper back from me. "And when Jerry told me that Daddy took out a missing persons report all those years ago, I didn't understand why it wasn't in the news back then. People are important. Lots of this stuff is just extras." She frowned at the paper.

"See, Momma, that's why I've been tryin' to find Bobby. Because he probably knows how Honcy, and eventually Joe, got that suitcase. And that money inside wasn't Aunt Jewel's. It couldn't have been. Mostly, I think he knows how she ended up in that field."

"You're right about that. Jewel didn't have a job. And I didn't know much about Bobby's family."

"Roland Thacker said something about them having an egg farm."

"Oh. . .the egg farm people." Momma picked up the stockpot of boiled rind and poured the rind into a strainer. The boiled water curled down the drain. "See, pour out and drain your rind. Then we'll stir the rind chunks into the sugar mixture after it sits for a few minutes."

"You started saying something about the egg farm?"

"The farm closed about twenty years ago, at least. I think the lady who lived there had a stroke or something. I don't know if her name was Johnson. We always called her Miss Edna. Papaw had known her husband at one time, and after he passed away, your Papaw used to go by and buy some of her eggs." Momma looked thoughtful. "You might want to check real estate transactions. Maybe you'll find the names of the former owners."

The spices on the stove smelled heavenly, sweet and tangy. My mouth watered as I turned to stir the mixture, now removed from the heat. "Momma, you're so smart. That was another lead I hadn't thought of."

"Baby girl, look at me." When I faced Momma, she grasped my shoulders. "Bobby Johnson is gone. And if he hurt Jewel, he probably didn't mean to. And if he's still alive, he's had all these years to live with knowin' what he's done. Put more time into your marriage and startin' a family, and let the past go. You've spent these last couple of weeks looking for a ghost."

"I'll try, Momma. But I can't promise you that. It's something I want to do for Aunt Jewel. To learn her full story so people can know. So our family can know."

"Some things we just need to leave alone. After her service, I'm done with grieving for Jewel. All your huntin' around won't bring her back to us." Momma took the boiled rind and stirred it into the syrupy mixture on the stove. "Now we let this cook some more. We cook the rind until we can just about see through it. Then we can it. Very simple."

I guessed as far as Momma was concerned, the subject of Bobby Johnson had just been closed. For good. By five o'clock, we had a few sealed glass jars of rind cooling, and I had a new skill. Maybe I'd can something else.

Although the county records office had closed for the day, I felt closer to finding Bobby after talking to Momma. I wished I could put my mental picture of young Bobby into a computer program that shows how people look when they age. If only I had an idea of his appearance now.

The watermelon field looked like a painting under the full moon, its leafy vines a grayish green with blackness underneath. I crouched at the edge of the woods, watching from behind a tree trunk. A couple faced each other in the field. A car, its engine chugging and lights out, waited by the main road. Old lady Flanders' farmhouse loomed across the driveway, its darkened windows looking like eyes observing the scene. A solitary light glowed on a pole in the farmyard. Its glow made a faint circle that faded before it reached the end of the drive.

"C'mon, you said you'd come with me." The young man had a sinewy build and a shock of hair that hid his face in shadow. *"But we've got to go tonight. And we can never come back."*

"All I want is to go away so I can marry you." The young woman, her light hair looking almost silver in the moonlight, clutched a flowered suitcase. *"But I've got to come back here. I'd miss my momma too much. I've got another niece or nephew comin' any day now. And little Andi-Candy wouldn't understand."* Her necklace glinted as it caught a speck of light from the farmyard.

Andi-Candy. Only one person had ever called me that. The old forgotten nickname made a wave of sorrow break over me as I watched, even as I knew what would happen next.

"Gimme the suitcase." Bobby reached, his hand like a claw.

"No." Jewel stepped back. *"This is wrong, and I ain't gonna be part of it. I won't do this to my family."* She continued skittering away from Bobby until she tripped over a watermelon and landed in the field.

"Get your hind ends in the car!" a familiar voice hollered from a distance.

"You ain't gonna run your mouth." Bobby stalked over to where Jewel scrambled to stand up. *"We've got a chance to start a new life, and you're coming, too."*

"Leave me alone, Bobby. I'm not going."

"Girl, if you don't get in that car, I'm gonna throw

you over my shoulder and stuff you in the backseat."
Bobby reached her in two more steps, kicking a
watermelon out of his way.

Jewel stumbled again, and this time Bobby pounced.
His hands reached for her neck, and he started dragging
her to the car—

I ran from the woods and onto the field, a scream
echoing in my ears—

"Baby?" I was in Ben's arms, and my drenched nightshirt stuck to my skin. "You screamed."

My bleary eyes took in the sight of my beloved bedroom, with a shirt hanging from the elliptical machine. No woods. No watching a drama I couldn't stop. I had a fluffy Spot-kitty on my feet. And Ben's warmth. I clung to him.

"I had an awful dream. It was about Bobby, and Jewel, and he was getting ready to hurt her. . . ." The shivers grabbed me despite my perspiration.

"Well, no wonder. You've been consumed with thinkin' about what happened to your aunt and trying to find Bobby."

"Ben, it was so real."

"Sometimes we work things through in our dreams. Or so I've heard."

I grabbed my robe to stop my shivering. "I didn't work anything out. Not really."

Ben shifted to a sitting position then swung his legs over the side of the bed. "I think we need to make you a cup of hot tea and talk."

Another confirmation of why I married this man. Some guys would have said, "Get over it, sweetheart, and go back to sleep."

I followed Ben to the kitchen and perched on one of the chairs while he filled the kettle with water. He poured himself a glass of juice. Spot joined us in the kitchen and paced, probably wondering why on earth we were up so late and not in our cozy bed where we belonged.

"This is partly my fault," Ben said.

"What are you talkin' about?" The shivers had subsided, and the comfort of our kitchen surrounded me. We'd selected that ceramic tile for the floor and laid it together, after having a spat over which pattern to use. That and the proper way to use a tile saw, even though neither of us had used one before. Why did people fight over unimportant things?

"You've done so much alone. You talked to Roland, Esther, Junker Joe—and found that suitcase. You called Honey's family and told your Papaw that one of his little girls is dead." Ben rubbed the stubble on his face. "It's been a big burden to carry. What have I done to help you?"

"Plenty. You found those shady deposits of Honey's. And you tried to see what Roland knew about them." I reached for his hand. "Besides, you've had the responsibility of running a business dumped on you. And someone attacked your reputation and our marriage. Plus, the restaurant lost one of its most dedicated employees. You helped me the other night, too, when you set up the video recorder. So if we're keepin' score, which I don't like to do, we're pretty much even."

The kettle started to rumble as the water heated.

Ben held up his hand. "I'll get your tea. Chamomile?"

I nodded. "With honey."

"How 'bout if I just stick my finger in the water to make it sweet?" Ben grinned as he took a cup down from the cabinet.

"You crack me up. Sure, whatever." What a man. He'd make a great father, too. Was my reluctance causing him pain? That would have to be for another discussion, another night. Already the dream about Jewel was fading. But the dream at the time had played like a movie in my mind.

"All this goin' on," Ben said as he carried my cup of tea to the table, "it's been weighing on you. And you've been handling it alone. When you don't have to."

No, I wasn't going to cry. Maybe he was right. "I haven't felt alone. Recently."

"I want to help you. What's next on your list? Who are you going to see next?"

"Momma said something the other day about the egg farm. Remember, it's down the road from here."

"I remember the place."

"I need to get its real estate records, who owns it now, and who used to own it. If the Johnsons ever lived there, maybe we can track them down somehow. And I was thinking, I'm sure Jerry has already run a background check on the name Bobby Johnson or Robert Johnson, just in Tennessee. Maybe something'll turn up." At this, I sighed. "It's almost like his name is Smith."

"You and I working on this together can do more than you running around on your own, exhausted." Ben clinked the ice around in his glass and took one more sip of juice. "I'll take the morning off and let Jonas run the kitchen. The county courthouse will have the property records. Another thing I thought of. I wonder if Gretchen's had money trouble. You remember that's why Honey didn't leave her anything in her will. She claimed Gretchen was always asking for money. I'll give Jerry a holler and see what he can find out. I imagine he's already looked for the Johnsons and already investigated Gretchen. But you won't have to work alone."

"Thank you. That's a good idea about Gretchen. She's extremely defensive, and I'd like to know why. Besides the fact that she was left out of what she sees as rightfully hers." The tea warmed me as it went down, and Ben's loving support warmed me, too.

"We've never tried to work as a team quite like this before, have we?"

"No, I guess we haven't. Not unless you count the kitchen tile. You'd think because we're married we'd know how."

"This is good practice for being a family."

"What do you mean?"

"When we have kids, we'll need to know how to work together."

"That's true, we will. I think we work pretty well together." But parenting wasn't like tiling a floor. It was a lifelong project, not a task completed in a week. Look at my grandparents. They'd raised both Jewel and Pearl the same way, and ended up losing Jewel. I could not imagine their anguish. Despite my earlier thoughts of wanting a little miracle in our lives, I found myself wavering. I didn't know if I could go through what my grandparents did with Aunt Jewel.

"I've been thinking. . ." He picked at the corner of a placemat.

Now was the time to tell him. "We've had a lot of changes in our lives in the past year. Change is stressful. I don't know if I want to have a baby right away. I'm not scared anymore, not like I used to be, anyway. I just think we'd be adding to everything we've gone through." My words felt like betrayal, especially considering my feelings during my conversation with Dr. Mukherjee the other night at the Watermelon Festival.

"Listen." Ben leaned closer. "I'm going to be forty in two years. Forty. I want to have time to *enjoy* my kids by the time we have them. And once they're out of the house, I want to have time to enjoy with you, as we keep growin' old together."

"I know you're almost forty. I'm right behind you." My tea didn't hold the same measure of comfort it had a few moments ago, but I gulped it down anyway.

"Then have faith in me. In us. In God's ability to help us be good parents. Life is all about change, darlin', and some things we shouldn't overanalyze. I think you're still scared, no matter how much you don't want to say so."

I couldn't say anything more. When Ben made speeches, I generally sat up and listened. But I didn't always like it when he was right.

Ben gave a yawn. "I'm goin' back to bed. I've got to be up in a few hours." He leaned toward me and kissed me, which only added to my feeling of shame. That probably wasn't his intention, but it happened anyway.

"I love you, Ben," I called after him as he left.

He stopped short and glanced at me over his shoulder. "I know. I love you, too."

15

The week crept along toward Saturday, the night of my big stake-out. Ben, true to his word as always, dug up some more information for me. County records revealed that the old egg farm had been owned by the Johnson family. Mr. Delmer Johnson had died in a car wreck in the late 1960s. Ben had discovered that bit of information on his own by checking newspaper archives.

Mrs. Edna Johnson supported the family through her chicken and egg business and small vegetable farm. Then in 1988 she sold the property and buildings to Roland Thacker. Curious, that Thacker would buy the property. He owned it still, along with a chunk of Tennessee riverfront.

All of these facts Ben produced when he stopped at the store Thursday afternoon. Since my bad dream, we hadn't talked about children. We continued to sidestep the issue, which was fine with me for now.

"I wonder where Mrs. Johnson went after she sold the farm." I concentrated on the soap mold in front of me as I poured the latest concoction into the bar-shaped blocks. Some people still liked simple glycerin bars with a hint of scent, so I always made sure to have a supply on hand. "You said Roland bought the Johnsons' property. That day I talked to him, he never mentioned it."

"Maybe he didn't think it was important."

"Maybe not." I slid the tray of molds down to the end of the table out of the way. "I told him I was trying to find the Johnsons, but he was in a hurry."

"I could always ask him what he knows." Ben leaned against the counter.

"You could, and he'll probably tell *you*." My back creaked from standing so long, and I stretched a little to work out the kinks. "Oh, but I'm tired."

"I'll give you a back rub while I tell you some even more interesting news that I learned."

"Here I am." I sat on my stool and turned my back to him. "Tell away."

Ben started working on my shoulders. My muscles screamed. "Wow, you're tense. Well, I did a search for Gretchen Wilkes. Found a notice of bankruptcy proceedings. This month, no less. The hearing is supposed to be next week."

"So she's going to court to declare bankruptcy." I felt the knots in my muscles dissolving. "I wonder if she assumed Honey would leave her some money."

"She probably did." Ben massaged my shoulder blades. "That is if she believed the old will was still valid. I imagine Honey's lawyer will know how many times her will was changed."

We called Robert Robertson's office and actually got through, then asked if Honey had any other earlier versions of her will.

"As a matter of fact, there are two of them, dated in the last year, no less." We heard rustling papers. "The first version of the will left the restaurant to Joseph Toms and Gretchen Wilkes. The second, dated just two months ago, left the restaurant to Mr. Toms alone. That's the one I mentioned to you at the reading. And you know about the third version."

"How old was that will?" I had to know.

"Ms. Haggerty filed this will six weeks ago, like I told you before."

"Thanks, Mr. Robertson." I glanced at Ben. "Is it possible for us to have copies of those?"

"They're void and worthless, but I suppose so. I'll have Suzie take care of it."

We hung up the phone. "I need to call Jerry," Ben said.

"Will that be enough to get Gabe freed?" I thought of his wife and baby.

"I don't know. Jerry probably knows about the former versions of her will. And they're probably building their case against Gabe. All a jury will need, though, is reasonable doubt."

"No wonder Joe was so mad at Honey for changing her will. It wasn't just us. It was that he'd been left out." With a few shoulder rolls, I realized Ben had gotten most of the kinks out of my back.

"I wonder what Joe and Gretchen have for alibis the night Honey was murdered."

"Considering the honesty issues people have had, I think if we asked them they wouldn't give us a straight answer."

I looked at the clock. "I need to see Papaw. I promised I would. Can you come with me?"

"Not today. I've got to head back to the restaurant."

"I'll see you later then. And thanks, honey, for

helping me." I had the fidgets and needed a change of scenery.

We said good-bye before Ben returned to the restaurant, and I locked up the store. I drove my Jeep out of town through Selmer, then Adamsville, and then headed north. In about twenty-five minutes, I saw the sign for Leisure Lodge. Papaw. I'd promised him I would come back. In the role reversal of parent and child, Momma tried to see Papaw twice a week at least, to make sure his clothes were in good repair and that he had all his shaving materials and toiletries. She visited and heard about what interested him.

When I entered the nursing home, I signed in at the desk like always. I found Papaw in his room, relaxing in his recliner and watching Jeopardy.

"I'm back, Papaw." I kissed him on the cheek, and his smile told me he'd again crisscrossed from present to past in his mind and wasn't sure where he was or when it was.

"Good, good. I'm glad to see you." He patted my hand. "Bobby came to visit the other day."

"Really?" I sank onto the quilt covering Papaw's bed. "To see you?"

"He walked right by my door, and I hollered at him. All he did was look at me and keep goin'. I wanted to ask him about my little girl, if he'd seen her." Papaw's hand shook as he held the remote.

"Mr. Kincaid, it's time for your medicine." A nurse wearing scrubs covered in a butterfly pattern entered the room. She carried a small paper cup of water and a smaller paper cup with pills. "Hi, there. Are you his family?"

"He's my grandfather. Has he seemed more confused lately?"

The nurse nodded. "He's talking to complete strangers, thinking they're family or friends. You have good days and bad days, right, Mr. Kincaid?"

Papaw used the water to wash the pills down. "Good and bad. Not sure how today is just yet, but I'm sure you'll be tellin' me if I don't remember."

I had to chuckle. He certainly hadn't lost his sense of humor. "Thanks, ma'am, for everything you do for Papaw."

"He's easy to help. A real charmin' man when he's not cranky. See you later, Mr. Kincaid." The nurse went out into the hall and on her way.

Maybe if Papaw traveled the past, he could help me learn more about Bobby. "Papaw, why didn't you like Bobby?"

"He's a slacker. All he does is sit around and play that fool guitar. A man can't put food on the table that way. His daddy would pitch a fit if he knew what's happened to his boy." Papaw shook his head. "His momma ain't going to hold onto that house, either. Her brother-in-law won't take 'em in if they lose the place."

"Who's her brother-in-law? Does he live around here?"

"Joe Toms. And that Bobby is going to end up like his uncle, a hand-to-mouth good-fer-nothin'."

"How can Joe be Bobby's uncle? Aren't they almost the same age?"

Papaw shrugged. "Bobby's momma was married to Joe's brother, Delmer. Joe must have been pretty young."

Great. Yet another someone conveniently left out information about Bobby Johnson. Joe, of course, had protected Honey and his *nephew*.

"All right!" Papaw's bellowed cheer made me jump. "Twenty-three thousand dollars. This guy's good." He pointed at the television screen.

I could tell I'd exhausted Papaw's trip to the past. But I think it brightened his day, and that would make Momma happy. "I'm goin' to leave now, Papaw."

"Okie-dokie, Andi girl." He chucked me on the shoulder. "You come back now. Don't be a stranger. I ain't gonna bite no one. Not if I can help it."

"You got it. Maybe next time Ben will come, too."

"I'll hold you to that."

―――

Friday night came. In a little more than twenty-four hours, I'd find out if our mystery visitor would come to the watermelon patch. To pass the time, I agreed to help Ben go through one of the storage rooms at Honey's Place. We crossed the darkened dining room. The last of the employees was cleaning the kitchen.

"We'll lock up when we leave," Jonas said as he pushed a stack of dirty dishes into the commercial dishwasher.

"Thanks. See you tomorrow afternoon." Ben headed into the office, with me trailing behind him. The restaurant's office held metal storage cabinets, a gargantuan desk, and stacks of restaurant equipment.

"Oh, Ben. How do you work in this?" I shook my

head. "I realize I'm not Ms. Neat-freak, but still. . ."

"It was worse, if you can imagine that." Ben moved to the back of the office and shoved some boxes away to expose a door. "Back here is where we're going to tackle. Or start, anyway."

The promise of a sneeze tickled my nose. "What in the world?"

Ben opened the door, and a stale smell filtered into the office. "I don't know when anyone last spent real time in this room." He flipped a light switch.

Boxes lined the room, each one with a year scribbled on the side. Nice. She organized in her own way, which really didn't help us much. "What are you going to do with all this?"

"I checked with Honey's lawyer. He said I couldn't throw anything away. We're still waiting to hear if anyone's contesting the will. But unofficially, anything older than ten years is safe to throw out." Ben moved to the first box. His speed amazed me. Maybe it's just when he's motivated, he moves faster. "This one says 1982."

It took us about an hour to shift decades' worth of boxes around, the newer ones to one side and the older ones to the other side of the room. A narrow path wound to the half a dozen strays, blank boxes we'd have to go through. Thankfully, two of them had "trash" scrawled on the sides in black marker.

"Who labels their trash?" I couldn't stop a giggle. Then came a sneeze. "Maybe Honey meant to dump this stuff."

"That's a possibility." Ben pulled the first box

toward him. "Let's see what she means by trash."

We both sank to our knees on the concrete floor, and Ben opened the box. "Newspapers. A bag of boxes for office equipment. Oh, lookie. The box for her adding machine. And the receipt."

I picked up the yellowed piece of paper. "Yup. 1978." I almost made a quip about that being a very good year, but 1978 was also when Jewel had disappeared. After fishing through the first box and finding nothing that smelled too bad, we started on the next one.

Ben paused before opening the box. Then he enveloped me in his arms and gave me a kiss that reminded me of how great it was to be married to him. Not the most romantic of places, but the restaurant storage room would do just fine.

"Wow," I said. He still held me in his arms. "That was unexpected."

He grinned. "That was the idea. 'Cause when do couples stop being newlyweds?"

I settled back on my heels. "Good question. Why does it take us more than five minutes of being alone before we realize it? Do people just stop noticing each other and what made them love each other in the first place? I don't mean just the attraction part of romance."

"Darlin', if you could figure that out, bottle, and sell it, we could retire next week."

"I can't believe how blind I was last summer. About getting married and settlin' down, I mean. Di told me how, sure, there'd be those ordinary days. But the joy of being with you makes up for the boring parts. Just like she said. And I don't want to lose that."

Ben looked down at the box. I wasn't sure if he was going to bring up the subject of a child again. I hoped not. I wanted to ease into things a little at a time.

"What's in this box?" I opened the second one marked trash, the box Ben had chosen before he kissed me. "Oh. Bank bags. And huge ones at that. Bigger than the ones you use now."

"These look old." Ben chuckled. "If Honey put these up for safekeeping, she sure forgot about them."

"I bet Di can ask her manager at the bank. Maybe they'll know what to do with them, especially since the bags say 'Property of State Bank of Tennessee.' Look, they've got registration numbers." The heavy cloth weighted down my lap. "The zippers are broken. And they're empty. No wonder Honey stuck these off to the side."

Another chuckle from Ben. "Honey probably thought the bank would charge her for them if she brought them in ruined."

I laughed then stopped. "Bank bags. A robbery the same weekend Aunt Jewel disappeared. Honey winning big at the gambling tables."

"And Bobby Johnson leaving town."

"But there's no telling how old these are, or how long they've been stuffed in the box. I'll talk to Di about the bags, and if there's anything suspicious, I'm sure they'll pass this along to Jerry."

We laughed over Honey being such a character and continued opening boxes. After two hours, the Dumpster outside the back door brimmed with trash.

We piled the three bank bags on the seat between us and drove home.

The next morning, I called Di with a bribe. If she came by the store on Monday morning, I'd have a tall café latte for her from Higher Grounds. That is, if she would take the bank bags to work with her.

"You found bank bags at Honey's?"

"Yeah, and they're pretty old. We were going through some of the stuff in a back room. You wouldn't *believe* the stacks of boxes."

"I'll come by and get them." Her voice had a weird tone to it.

"What is it?"

"Are they from our branch?"

"I'm not sure. State Bank of Tennessee, they say on the outside." I read aloud as I held one of the bags. "I didn't think we should throw them away. Ben said maybe Honey didn't want to get charged for them because the locks are broken."

"Okay."

When Di got tight-lipped, I'd learned not to try to drag anything out of her. It would keep until Monday. And if she didn't mind, I probably would go to the bank with her, too.

The Saturday hours crept along as I kept the store open and worked on soaps. Summertime did that to my schedule. If I had my way, I'd be at the river or the city pool with the rest of the crowd, cooling off. The hot air made my neck prickle, my pony tail doing little to help me, and the window air-conditioning unit in the salesroom window chugged along. But the box fan blowing cooler air from the sales floor to my workroom didn't help much.

I reached home a little after five. Ben had made plans to catch a ball game over at Jerry's, so he'd be out late. And I'd be sure to make a show of having lights-out at nine before sneaking out to the shed. I found the digital camcorder on the coffee table in the living room. If I could record the event—providing someone showed up—I'd have something to show Jerry.

Spot complained about me neglecting her. She romped around my ankles as I crossed into the kitchen. Ben knew what he was doing, giving me a kitten who somehow had almost tripled in size in the last month or so. My poor forlorn kitten proved how over-busy I'd made myself. How could I pay attention to a baby, who would require more attention than any pet? Not that I didn't want to care for a baby.

Ben would say it was me being too hard on myself and giving up too easily.

"Lord, I thought I'd learned that lesson last summer. Of not letting fear of failing make me give up." You couldn't send back a child, no matter how much I'd begged Momma to send Di back when she was a baby. "I do want a baby, I do. And Ben was right, I'm scared."

Maybe admitting my fears would help God enable me to conquer them. After all, *He* probably wasn't surprised.

Okay. I thought I knew how to operate the camera correctly. I filmed Spot playing with a scrap of paper on the kitchen floor and that went well. She rolled onto her gray-and-white back and mewed at me in her kitty-cat voice. I stopped recording and played with her for a while.

Finally. Nine p.m. I slipped on my navy blue nylon wind suit. I couldn't very well go outside with my tuna-white legs glowing in the light of the moon once the sun set. The moon had passed the full phase but still had enough shine to illuminate the yard. All the lights were out inside the house. Spot knew something was up, because she kept trying to trip me in the way that cats do. But nothing was going to keep me from my stakeout.

The night air prickled outside, the last touch of dusk to the west disappearing. My wind suit stuck to my legs and made me feel as if I'd done a round of circuit training at Shapers. Which reminded me, I needed to go back again and see how Vivian was doing.

With flashlight and camcorder in hand, I crept to the shed. A rustling noise, too close to be a breeze in the treetops, made me pause. I turned round in the yard. Nothing I could see. The wooden shed loomed in front of me. I shuddered. The romance and coziness was gone, without Ben here. The shed's open door yawned like a dark tunnel.

I flipped on the flashlight and breathed easier. The riding lawnmower waited with its cushioned seat. I could sit on that and still have a glimpse through the knothole Ben made. Everything else looked normal.

No creatures waited to attack once I turned out the light.

Waiting does not come easily for me. Ben, on the other hand, has plenty of patience in the fruit of the Spirit department. This is probably why God usually gives me plenty of opportunities to wait, and to learn self-control, too.

So I listened. I heard the breeze sweeping through the woods—*please, Lord, a little rain would help beat the heat tonight*. Then a few crickets chimed in from their hideouts closer to the river.

I heard a rustling again. My heart pounded. I leapt from the riding mower and looked out the knothole to get a better view of a perfectly ordinary watermelon field.

A faint mew sounded from the corner where Ben kept the weed eater.

"Spot." Great. My shadow had followed me from the house.

She let me catch her and I scooped up her warm furriness. "Every time you get outside you get *me* into trouble."

If I hurried, I'd have enough time to toss her in the house and get back to my lookout inside the shed. Just as I moved to step into the yard, I froze.

I heard a car coming up the drive.

16

The car stopped at the edge of the driveway, and the driver turned off the headlights. I cradled Spot in my arm and tiptoed back to the mower to grab the camcorder.

Then came the faint click of a car door. Footsteps. I couldn't breathe. Spot squirmed. At least she couldn't bark at him. I moved so I could see through the knothole Ben had drilled the other night. A dark figure stood at the edge of the watermelon patch then crossed onto the field and went to stand where Spot and I had discovered the body. He hunched over as if looking for something. I'd seen that stance before, one stormy night in the driving rain.

The face was lost in the shadow of a ball cap as whoever it was turned to face the shed. I didn't make a noise that I could tell, but Spot's claws had started gouging into my wind suit. Fine. I let the cat go. She scurried into the darkness. Something clattered to the ground.

The man moved closer, and I fought the urge to run. If I stayed quiet, maybe he'd think Spot was running loose on her own. Did he intend to do to me what he'd done to Jewel? Maybe this wasn't such a great idea. Why didn't I think of this before? Ben would be furious. Besides, I hadn't actually planned to talk to the guy. Just film him and take it to Jerry. *Oh, Lord, what was I thinking? What if he hurts me, too, whoever he is?*

And Ben's not home.

A few more steps. Just as I decided to dart around the corner and shine my flashlight on his face, he clicked *his* flashlight on. Straight at the knothole and into my eye.

"What do you want from me?"

I couldn't place the voice. Had I heard it while shopping in Value-Mart, or dining at Honey's Place, or anywhere else around town? My eye teared up from the sudden brightness.

"The truth." I shrank back from the hole.

"I loved her. What happened was unintentional. Never wanted things to go that far."

All I heard was crickets and the beating of my heart.

"And I've had to live with what I'd done. Didn't think the past would come back with a vengeance. Honey and her kind have long memories."

He turned away.

"Bobby, did you kill Honey, too?"

The man broke into a run. I followed, tripping over whatever it was that Spot had knocked down. I skittered around the corner of the shed, my flashlight in hand. I clicked it on. The light made wild arcs across the field and on the driveway. All I saw was the back of his head, a T-shirt, and some jeans. Dark sneakers.

He reached the idling car parked at the end of the tree-lined driveway and jumped inside. The flashlight slipped from my hand. Bobby—it had to be him—sped off in his darkened car.

I trudged back to the shed. Working out at Shapers

had helped me find more energy, but I had a way to go in the physical fitness department. I couldn't have chased him down even if I'd been foolish enough to try. Once I found the camcorder in the shed, I headed for the house. Spot waited for me on the back step. She'd had enough of her romp outside, and so had I. My pulse still pounded.

Inside the kitchen, I let Spot scamper across the tile floor to her water bowl. Then I sank onto a chair. The answering machine blinked, so I checked the messages. Ben had called. I dialed Jerry's number.

"Hey, were you in the shower when I called just a few minutes ago?"

"Um, no. I set up a stakeout in the shed."

"You what?"

"You weren't here, so I figured if it looked like we'd gone out, maybe Bobby would show."

"That was a dangerous thing to do."

"I know, I know. I realized that as soon as a car showed up. Don't worry, though. He ran off. I'm fine."

"I'll be home in ten minutes, babe, and you can tell me all about it."

"I'll make a fresh pitcher of iced tea. This wind suit has me feelin' like I've been sittin' in a sauna."

True to his word, Ben arrived home ten minutes later. I poured us each a glass of tea and we took our seats on the porch swing, a wedding gift from Di and Steve. Part of me wanted us to spend every evening on the porch, drinking iced tea and listening to the night.

"Imagine that. All that lookin', and he really is

here in the area somewhere." Ben gazed out into the yard that ended in a strip of trees and then the main road. "He has to be, if he reads the *Dispatch*."

"I know." My bare legs thanked me for exchanging the wind suit for a pair of cutoffs. A soft breeze cooled the night. "But it got me to thinking."

"Uh-oh. That's dangerous."

"Very funny." For that, he deserved a poke in the ribs.

"Ow."

"As I was saying, I was thinking. About something Bobby said. He told me her death was an accident, that he hadn't meant things to go that far, and he loved her. He's had to live with what he'd done all these years. Plus, Honey and her kind had long memories."

"So Honey probably *was* blackmailing him." Ben pushed off the porch floor with his foot and set the swing in motion again. "Interesting."

"But, and this is just a guess, I don't think Bobby killed Honey."

"Are you sure? Remember the talk of his temper. And whoever killed Honey made sure they finished the job. Blackmail is a strong motive for murder."

"I know that." I also knew that after the police had released the crime scene at the restaurant, Ben had cleaned the kitchen himself, refusing to allow any of the other employees help him. He hadn't wanted the other employees, especially Esther, to see what Honey's attacker had left behind.

Despite the humidity, I leaned closer to Ben. He kissed the top of my head. "Tonight, though, Bobby didn't sound angry. He seemed more. . .beaten. My gut tells me that if he'd killed Honey he wouldn't have talked to me and then run off when I called him Bobby. He would have repeated what happened at the restaurant."

My own words made me shiver. How foolish I'd been, trying to draw a killer out.

"I don't want to think about that happening." Ben's voice sounded low and somber. "I should have stayed home tonight and skipped the game. And you should have told me what you were plannin'. Bobby probably came out here all those other times late at night, even while we were home, and we never knew it. If he'd seen my truck, it wouldn't have mattered. Because he probably wouldn't have cared if we were both at home. Promise me you won't do anything like that again."

"That's an easy to promise make. I'm so sorry." The tea cooled my throat. "What next, though? I know Bobby is here somewhere, but I think if I try again to find him, he'll disappear again."

"We'll tell Jerry about what happened tonight, and your theory about the killer." His arm tightened around me.

"And he might tell me that Gabe is still in custody and they have their man." I frowned and swirled the ice cubes around in my glass, just like the thoughts swirled inside my head.

"If that's true, and Gabe's innocent, we still have a murderer on the loose who thinks he's getting away with it."

I looked out at the night and silently prayed for

wisdom and fresh ideas. Like the darkened woods across the road, the unanswered questions lay before us. And now maybe I'd sent Bobby back into hiding, this time for good.

———

Monday morning came, and I waited at the store for Di to arrive. I hoped she'd arrive before her latte got cool. Mine tasted great, as usual. Trudy had found her calling in the coffee world. Now that the Watermelon Festival was over, I decided to revive my morning ritual of cruising by Higher Grounds.

I'd already planned out my day by making a list on my trusty notepad. During some earlier moments of distraction, I'd poured soap the color of autumn leaves into the Christmas tree molds. Those definitely wouldn't even make it onto my clearance shelf in the store room. My supply inventory needed replenishing. Then I decided to plan a harvest party night. Since I was an official member of the Chamber, I could have an open house and include fellow Chamber members on the guest list. Maybe we could turn it into a charity event as well.

A frantic banging on the front door made me look up. On the other side, Di pounded the glass. Her eyes looked round. She tapped her watch. I moved to unlock the door.

"Sorry I'm running late this morning. Taylor wet the bed last night. I think he's upset about moving." Di streamed into the shop. "Where are the bank bags?"

"Right here." I picked them up and pointed at the counter. "And there's your coffee."

I had a hard time keeping up with Di as she sped along ahead of me to the bank. She turned her van into the bank parking lot, circled the employees' only area, and found an empty space.

Once I found a space myself, I joined Di at her van and told her what had happened Saturday night. "So that's why I think there's a killer out there. Ben warned me to be careful, and I don't blame him. When I think of what could have happened. . ."

"But nothing bad happened, and God had His hand on you."

"He did. So many times we're protected in spite of ourselves, and we don't realize it." Then I sighed. "What about Honey, though? If only she had known she was in trouble. Or that someone else was at the restaurant with her that night. Like Junker Joe. . ."

"I know. It seems to me that they pinned her murder on Gabe a little too quickly. I mean, I know they had evidence and all. But still. . ." Di took the bags from me, and I picked up her coffee. "The office isn't open yet, but I think my manager will let you come inside for a few minutes."

She punched in her code for the employee entrance, and I followed her into the bank. We passed by a break room full of snack machines and a soda machine. Di greeted some coworkers, who looked at the bank bags and me with quizzical expressions.

Her manager let us into her paneled office. I vaguely recalled seeing her at the Chamber of Commerce meeting. The woman's crisp suit made her look like she'd stepped out of the Trump Tower in New York.

We shook hands. "Ms. Hartley, good to see you. What do you have for us?" The manager looked at the bags that Di clutched.

Di shot me a look and placed the bank bags on her manager's desk. "Well, it's these bags."

"My husband and I found them in a storage room at the restaurant. Honey's Place. We thought they looked pretty old. And, um, the locks are broken."

She picked up one bag and turned it over in her hands. "We keep track of all bags, according to customer and bank branch. I'm not sure how Ms. Haggerty got these bags, but I have a suspicion. These are the ones we receive from our armored couriers and use in transfers. And just looking at the number sequence, these aren't our bags. They're from another branch. Customers don't normally receive these kinds of bags. What kind of bag does the restaurant use now?"

"I think they use navy blue plastic zippered bags. Ben drops one off every night and picks up an empty one."

"Did you find anything inside the bags?" She sounded hopeful.

"No. They were empty."

"Well, thank you for returning these." The manager had a look on her face as if her thoughts had wandered elsewhere and she wasn't about to tell us where they'd traveled. "Can we reach your husband at the restaurant today?"

"Ben will be there all day until six," I said. "We wanted to make sure the bank got these back."

"Again, thank you. If we need you, we'll be in touch." The manager picked up her phone and ended our little meeting.

Di and I left her office and stopped in the break room so she could finish her latte before the bank opened. The smell of fresh brewing coffee filled the room, but we both had tall cups of the good stuff from Higher Grounds. I caught a few glances of envy as employees trickled into the room to place their lunches in the refrigerator.

"Have you been house hunting yet?" I decided I might as well broach the subject of Di, Steve, and the boys moving a whole hour away from us.

"We're going this weekend. Actually, I think we're going to rent for now until we get a feel for the neighborhoods." Di sipped her latte. "We're also going to take the boys to see some of the sights in Jackson. If we're, um, uprooting from Greenburg, we should try to find family activities for us to do there. Stevie is heartbroken. He's going to miss football this fall, plus baseball in the spring."

"It's going to be weird without you here." I frowned. "Is Stevie going to try some sports up in Jackson? Of course they've got football and baseball."

Di nodded. "We've told him that. It's just going to take adjusting to not being here. I told him we have our cell phones, e-mail, and visiting on weekends. Plus you and Ben can come visit us. It's not like we'll be in another state or hours and hours away."

"I know. But you've always been around here." No way would I sigh and add to Di's doldrums. Moving from the town you'd always lived in had to be hard. "How are Momma and Daddy doing?"

"Daddy's taking it in stride. Momma's been thinkin' about the service for Aunt Jewel." Di walked to the trash can and tossed her paper cup away then returned to sit across from me. No matter how I looked at it, my sister probably felt guilty for bringing up moving, especially with the renewed grief of losing Aunt Jewel all over again. At least it seemed that way.

"Don't feel bad, Di. You and Steve had to tell us at some point. Better than right before you leave. Momma and Daddy would definitely be plenty more upset. . ."

"More upset than they are now? I know I said Daddy's taking it all right, but he's been calling. Our daddy. On the phone."

Daddy is not a phone sort of guy. He uses monosyllables as much as possible and sounds like he's about to take someone out to the woodshed. And that's just when ordering pizza. I pondered our lives and the changes we'd encountered in a matter of weeks.

"I can't believe Aunt Jewel's service is Thursday. This sounds kind of bad, but I'll be glad when it's over with. Do you think many people will come?" Ben and I hoped so, for Momma's sake.

"I don't know. I'm just glad Momma's getting some closure."

I nodded then picked up my coffee and stood. "That's what I'm grateful for, too. Well, I guess I'd better go. I need to open the store now so I can get used to when Sadie's away at college. I've been spoiled having her here this summer, being able to leave when I need to."

"Hey, one more thing." Di's expression stopped me. "I meant to ask earlier, but how are you and Ben doing?"

"Good." I looked away and took my seat again. "Better sounds more accurate. Not that we've really had problems. I mean, we're still newlyweds."

"Newlyweds adjusting to being around each other all the time. Plus, those pictures you received in the mail had to be a shock."

"They were. Ben and I had a good talk, and we definitely crossed over that road bump. Of course, the pictures themselves didn't tell the whole story." I paused and sipped what was left of my latte. "Do you. . .do you love Steve differently now? I mean. . .do you really love him more, like they *say* love grows? Whoever *they* are. Ben and I spent so long dating while being apart lots of the time, and now. . ."

"You're feelin' like you're tripping over each other?"

"Not exactly. We spend just as much time apart as we did when he was on the road, only now we live in the same house and he comes home to sleep every night. I just thought it would be different somehow. Almost feels like we're turning into an old married couple sometimes." Another bank employee came in, greeted Di, and poured herself a cup of coffee.

Only after the other woman left did Di reply. "It's always different. Love changes as it grows. I think sometimes we have higher expectations than we really should."

Di's remark made me chuckle. "So I should just get myself some lowered expectations, huh?"

She blushed. "I didn't mean you ought to lower your expectations, like marriage is all downhill after you say, 'I do.' It's just that you see someone every day, at their best and worst. Did Ben know about your, um, cooking skills?"

"Yes and no. Before we got married, I would cook him one of the two recipes I can make. Instead of going out on a date, I always stuck to what was easy for me. Or else Ben would use the grill at his house, or we'd go out to eat when he was home from the road. . ."

"Oh, I wish we could go out to eat more often." Di almost sounded jealous. "Enjoy that while you can. It's more expensive once the kids come along, especially when they're too old for kid meals. Oops, don't want to discourage you in that area, either."

"You're not discouraging me," I admitted. "I'm just going back and forth on the idea. Starting a family is a big decision. I finally met Dr. Mukherjee, the new OB in town, at the Watermelon Festival last weekend. She talked about what a miracle each life is. Part of becoming a parent sounds wonderful. To participate in a miracle and watch your child grow into who God wants him to be. What a gift. And responsibility."

"She sounds like a neat doctor."

I nodded. "But then, look at what happened to Aunt Jewel. Just read between the lines. She went wild. I can't imagine the heartbreak a parent must go through. Think of Papaw. And Nana, too. You know Momma and Aunt Jewel probably went to church three times a week, plus summer Bible school for kids, plus Papaw reading devotions. Momma and Aunt Jewel ate, drank, and slept what Nana and Papaw taught them."

"We both know the day comes when kids have to decide what they believe and what they don't. I keep hearing that bein' a mom is all about learning how to let go." Di frowned. "Stevie's already getting to that age where I can tell he'll be a handful as a teenager. Almost twelve, and he already thinks he knows everything. And strong opinions? On one hand, that's insurance against peer pressure. To a point. But in another way that worries me, that he'll fight us even though we know what's best for him. Steve and I are sticking together regarding the kids, but that doesn't keep me from gettin' on my knees every night and praying that we do the right thing."

"Wow. You're sure convincing me to have a whole brood." At this rate, adopting a puppy or getting a little kitten sister for Spot sounded a lot better than giving birth to a new little human.

17

I shouldn't have been surprised when Robert Robertson called Ben at work Tuesday morning. As expected, Gretchen Wilkes had somehow hired her own lawyer and contested the will. This, in effect, froze all of Honey's assets. Ben could only draw his own regular salary but wasn't free to sell her property or reap more of the restaurant's profits. Like the place raked in the cash or something.

The Haggerty genes ran pure through Gretchen, with her penchant for revenge. But Ben seemed content to run the restaurant as before. We renewed our determination to place the future of the restaurant in God's hands, reminding ourselves that we were in His hands, as well.

The phone rang just as I checked the temperature on my next batch of soap. When I was in the middle of my concoctions, I didn't have time to stop and chat. Plus, I had to act when the temperature reached the correct point. The Tennessee River Soaps answering machine echoed from the niche that held my desk. No official news yet from Di about the bank bags, although the bank manager had called Ben yesterday morning at the restaurant, probably to see if our stories matched. Of course she'd suspected the bank bags had been stolen.

"Andromeda, it's Momma. The nursing home called. Your Papaw attacked a visitor today."

I made it to the phone in a few steps. "I'm here. Sorry. I was in the middle of something. What happened? Who'd Papaw attack?"

Momma sounded tired. "A visitor came. Papaw thought he was Bobby. He got a few punches in before they got him off the man. They've called his doctor, who's going to adjust his medicines."

"Oh, Momma."

"So I'm asking you this one time only. Leave the thing with Bobby be. It's only causing trouble. For all of us. Look at your Papaw, even being questioned about Jewel. My daddy might have had a quick temper, but he never raised his hand to us unless our hind ends needed a swat or two when we were little. "

After apologizing again, I hung up the phone. Poor Momma. I couldn't imagine having to put one of my parents in a home and prayed we'd never have to make that decision. All I'd wanted to do was help my family by finding Bobby Johnson. Even though Momma was upset, I knew deep down she probably craved answers, as I did. Which is why I couldn't stop searching, despite Jerry's assertion that there was no connection between the murders, and the fact that Gabe was already in custody.

I sank down onto my stool in the workroom. "Lord, I've been running around like crazy here, trying to find the man who killed my aunt. It's not even about revenge, but more about letting my momma have the chance to talk to him. Or, I don't know what I was looking for. Maybe I've been searching for Aunt Jewel somehow. Sounds weird, I guess. But Lord, You're not surprised. The little girl who never got to say good-bye wants a chance to do that."

I got my chance Thursday morning. We all did. Momma had planned a simple service, and the pastor of her little country church said a few words at the cemetery. Ben kept his arm around me the whole time. Di, Steve, and the boys stood next to us. Momma and Daddy, too. Plus Jerry and Trudy and even Sadie came. Nearly two dozen of our friends. A lone vehicle was parked about one hundred yards down the sloping hill from us, its occupant watching our gathering.

After the pastor said the final "amen," we waited a respectful distance while Momma said good-bye.

Greenburg Memorial Park is an outdoor sanctuary, with a green carpet and a ceiling that ends at heaven's doors, somewhere far beyond us. I felt the whisper of a breeze touch my cheek and go along its way. Somewhere a bird sang. When I was younger, the idea of row upon row of cold carved stone made me shiver. But the older I get, the more I realize the significance of Ecclesiastes 3. A time for everything under heaven. A time to be born. . .I touched my stomach and thought of the single line in the window of the pregnancy test.

And a time to die. Rows of stones stretched beyond us to where our vehicles waited. *It's being apart that's so hard, Lord. All the might-have-beens and could-have-beens with Aunt Jewel. I know you can make this work for good for all of us.*

The crest of the small hill gave a good view beyond the park, to the pines and oak that studded the countryside at the edge of Greenburg.

"Ain't it gorgeous, Andi-Candy?" I could almost hear Aunt Jewel say.

I snapped my attention back to our little group. Trudy was talking to Momma in low tones. Momma nodded then addressed all of us. "Trudy's invited us to Higher Grounds. She's prepared some sandwiches and ordered some other food in. Plus, she says, all the coffee you can drink."

Momma smiled and squeezed Trudy's hand. "Thank you, thank you so much. I. . .I honestly hadn't planned anything other than the service."

Ben and I joined them at the edge of the narrow drive that wound its way through the park. "Trudy. Thank you."

"It's a shame Greenburg didn't do more." Trudy shook her head. "We all can stick our noses in where we're not wanted—or needed—around this town, and other times we pretend we don't see what's goin' on around us because we don't want to get involved."

I realized then that I didn't know what Trudy believed, or if she believed like I did. But I did know her words rang true scripturally. We were all so busy straining out gnats and swallowing camels. It was easy to pick at someone's faults and ignore the more important issues.

Jerry and Ben chatted near a tree, and I joined them. Jerry was shaking his head.

"Andi Hartley, Ben just told me what you did the other night."

"Oh, my stakeout." My face flamed at the recollection. As much as my gut told me I had nothing to fear from Bobby Johnson, what if he *had* tried something? "I'm not doing anything like that again, believe me."

"I can't believe the setup worked," Jerry said.

"I just hope that reporter at the *Dispatch* doesn't cause problems for you," I admitted.

"What's his name?"

"Travis Bush."

"He must be Fleta's kin. Her daughter married one of the Bush boys from Savannah." Jerry scratched his chin then tugged at his belt loop. "I'll talk to her. We put a little pressure on him, he won't overstep."

We all made our way to our separate vehicles. The guys walked ahead of Di and me, while the two of us walked arm in arm along the narrow drive.

"I can't believe y'all are leaving in two weeks." I tried not to sound droopy.

"Stop. I don't want to cry." Di squeezed my arm. "The bank agreed to my job transfer, did I tell you?"

"No." I struggled to find the right words. "Life is all about change. You said parenting is about letting go. I realized by hangin' onto that quest for Bobby Johnson, part of me was trying to hang onto Aunt Jewel. But she's not here anymore. I'd like to think she's with Jesus."

"Me, too. We'll find out one day, won't we?"

"I know we will." Maybe with Aunt Jewel reconsidering about leaving Greenburg, she'd made her peace with God and knew running off with Bobby would have been a mistake.

We reached our vehicles that made a winding line

along the driveway. I froze when I reached the door of our truck.

The other vehicle remained downhill from us, the driver still leaning against the door. If the visitor's interest lay closer to his car, he wouldn't be staring up the gentle hill at us. Not for so long. If he were any other resident of Greenburg, he'd have joined the group, even if he had come out of curiosity and not because of our family. Bobby?

I gave a small wave. The driver raised his hand almost like a salute, and then climbed into his vehicle and drove away. Blue car. Not much that stood out about it. I figured I should start carrying Ben's binoculars with me. Whoever it was had worn a ball cap—I couldn't tell if it was black or dark blue—a simple T-shirt, and blue jeans. He could have been any of a number of men in the area.

Bobby Johnson, I just don't know if I can leave you alone.

T he bank just called," Ben's voice came across the phone, and the tone of his voice made me sit down at my work desk Friday morning. "Those bags we found? Well, their numbers matched the ones counted missing after the bank robbery in Selmer. Thirty years ago."

"We need to talk to Jerry, if the bank hasn't called him already."

"I don't know that this would be in the Greenburg PD's hands, especially the amount of money stolen. But he'd sure be able to tell us what happens next."

"How much was stolen in the robbery?"

"Over two hundred thousand dollars."

"Honey and Bobby. It's got to be them. But the whole town knows and believes the story about Honey winning at the casinos in Bossier City years ago, and opening the restaurant. If Bobby helped her, that explains how that money ended up in Aunt Jewel's suitcase."

"We can talk to Jerry about all of that."

Jerry met us at the restaurant, and the three of us had lunch in Ben's office. Ben said we didn't want to draw attention to our conversation by eating in the main dining room, although the *Greenburg Dispatch* would probably hunt down the story. And the nice cub reporter who sold me the classified ads would find himself possessing a wonderful opportunity to snag a front-page scoop. I don't know if that would help the investigation of Honey's killer or hinder it.

We told Jerry about finding the bank bags and turning them over to the bank, plus reminded him about the cash in Aunt Jewel's suitcase.

"I heard from the bank about the bags," Jerry said around a mouthful of his grilled chicken sandwich. Not fried. The guy definitely was eating healthier than I'd ever seen him eat. I'd have to point that out to Ben, who probably didn't notice at all.

I took a sip of iced tea. "I wanted to have some evidence for you. The trail of Aunt Jewel's killer was pretty stale. And Honey's fresher case had priority. But we're pretty sure that Bobby's somewhere in the local area. Maybe he's got an alias or he lives off the grid. You know. Pays cash. No accounts in his name."

"Could be." Jerry scratched his chin. "I'm not involved in the bank matter now. The Selmer bank is in McNairy County, and we're in Hardin County."

"Jerry, I think you arrested the wrong guy. Gabe's no murderer."

"Oh, so you know Gabe? Well enough to know about his flimsy alibi?" Jerry's neck hairs bristled. Or that's what it looked like, anyway. "We have evidence that he was there that night."

"No, I don't know him," I said. "But a young married man with a little girl isn't going to throw his life away by killing someone. Gabe's a survivor. He was workin' two jobs when Honey fired him. That much I do know. Right, Ben?" I glanced at my husband. He'd already cleared through his burger and was working on the fries.

"You're right."

"Could you please say that again?"

"You're right." Ben winked at me.

I sighed and looked at Jerry. "I love it when that happens. But seriously, what's happened to Gabe? Where is he now?"

"He's at the county lockup. He's waiting for arraignment and then probably a trial date if the DA gets his way."

"Where's his family?" I thought of Maryann and Zoë.

Jerry ate the last bite of his sandwich. "They're with her relatives. I'm sorry her husband wasn't just a hardworking guy whose employer did him wrong. You know as well as I do that revenge can cause the nicest people to do the unthinkable."

He had a point there, and I couldn't argue with him. I well remembered the morning in the restaurant when Gabe had literally stormed in and we'd been afraid he had a gun. Still, I didn't like the idea of Gabe being a murderer. I preferred to think of him as a desperate young man trying to take care of his family. Yet Melinda Thacker had possessed a sweet exterior, and she'd murdered her own sister last summer. But the sweetness burned off because of her rage within.

"Do you have enough to arrest Bobby Johnson, should you find him?" Ben asked.

"From what you've told us, we have enough to question him about Honey, especially given their history. Blackmail would be hard to prove, but if she was draggin' out the past, that would incriminate her, too." A loud clatter echoed from the kitchen outside, and Jerry jerked his head toward the door. "Especially if Honey knew he killed Jewel and helped him bury the body in the field. If he's as remorseful as you said he sounded, he might confess."

"What are you doing?" A stern voice sounded from the kitchen area. "Only employees can come back here."

Ben stood. "That's Jonas. I'd better check it out."

Honey's Place has always been a home-style restaurant, but that didn't mean people could just make themselves at home.

"So, Jerry, about Gabe—"

"Look who Jonas found listening outside the door." Ben herded a familiar-looking lanky young man into the office.

"You work for the *Dispatch*." I pointed at him. "Why didn't you just knock on the office door and ask to talk to us? Or call for an interview?" The reporter shrank from my glare. Maybe the "momma look" came naturally. My momma would be proud something maternal rubbed off on me.

"Because he knows I'm not going to give out details of an investigation with him right here." Jerry got to his feet, and the room seemed a lot smaller with the two men staring at the reporter. The kid fumbled with his pen and notepad, licked his lips, and I imagine he wondered how fast the other two men could run.

A thought smacked me in the forehead. "I know why you're sniffing around. You knew I took those ads out, Honey's old ads. And you knew she'd been murdered. So you thought you'd trail along to see what else you could learn." I should have known that the eager glint in his eyes when I'd seen him at the newspaper office meant he craved a story. I'd figured he'd given up on the idea. But now, to find him lurking around and skulking in corners? He could do better than that.

The young man bobbed his head. He must have had his hair trimmed, because it didn't flop into his eyes like it did when I was at the newspaper. "There's a big story here somewhere. It could put Greenburg on the map. A thirty-year-old murder. A new victim, the owner of Greenburg's best restaurant. A tortured lost love who's out there, somewhere, living with his guilt."

"And it could boost your career, too." Jerry had a pretty decent glare of his own.

"I'm tired of getting kicked over to the classifieds desk when the paper needs help. I went to the state college, got a journalism degree, and I've got student loans to repay. So far I haven't heard from any of the larger papers about a job." The young man shrugged. "Can you blame me for trying to get noticed?"

"What was your name again?" Jerry asked.

"Travis Bush."

"Oh, you're Fleta's grandson. Let me think about this. You've found the human interest angle to this case, and I can't say it ain't interestin'." Jerry took his seat again.

"You can interview my momma." I couldn't believe I'd just opened my mouth and heard those words come out. "And, um. . .maybe the man we're looking for will read it, and. . ."

"Have a change of heart? Come clean?" Jerry

shrugged. "It might work. But I'm not sharing any details of the case. Check your own news archives, Travis. The facts of the case haven't changed. So don't think you can drag any new details out of the police. And I'm not sayin' there's a connection between Jewel Kincaid's murder and Harriet Haggerty."

"Bobby seemed really sorry that night he showed up at the watermelon field and talked to me." At that, Travis's head perked up like a hound catching a scent, and he looked at me.

"Sorry he got caught was probably more like it," said Ben.

"Believe it or not, I do want to help. And not just to get a good story." Travis smiled. He brushed some imaginary wayward hair out of his eyes. "But because it's the right thing to do. I liked Honey Haggerty. I liked her pies, too."

I wanted to believe him despite his overeager manner. "You sound convincing. But part of this is my family's story. I could give you my momma's phone number."

Jerry cleared his throat. "I'd like to see that story before you run it."

"I'm not going to blow your investigation or anything. All I ask is one thing." What a charmer. I bet the girls nearly fell into his blue eyes. Too bad they wouldn't work on Jerry.

"What's that?" Jerry remained as impassive as a rock.

"Release Gabe Davis." Travis flashed a grin.

At that, Jerry let loose with a chuckle. "You might

be Fleta's grandson, but you've got a lot to learn about the law. Even if I wanted to, I couldn't release him. It's out of my hands. I can present everything we've talked about to the DA, but I can't go up to County Jail and turn the key."

"When I write this story, Mrs. Hartley, I promise you I'll do right by your family."

"I'll let you tell that to my momma." I started to write her number down then stopped. "Let me call her first and explain. She wanted me to drop my search for Bobby."

"Okay. You know where to find me." At that, Travis left the way he'd come. We all looked at each other.

"I have to check on the kitchen." Ben glanced through the doorway Travis had just crossed through.

"And I need to get back to the store. Plus call Momma."

Ben gave me a quick kiss then nodded at Jerry. "Come on by the house sometime. Don't be a stranger."

"Aw, I'd only be in the way."

"Really, Jerry, we should make plans to have you come for dinner. I promise I won't burn anything. This time," I said. "Before you know it, Thanksgiving will be here." And Di would have already moved away. . .

"Let me know if or when Travis interviews your momma."

"I will. Do you think it'll do any good?" I tried not to hope.

"It might. Sort of like Crime Stoppers. But not exactly. We can't afford to give a reward or anything.

And for the moment, we have someone in jail for one of the crimes." Jerry picked up his lunch wrapper and tossed it in a trash can.

We entered the bustle of the kitchen and tried to keep out of the way. Ben orchestrated the kitchen symphony. Jonas was back at his spot as prep cook. Esther seated customers. She nodded at me as I left. Now I had to break the news to Momma that Aunt Jewel's story wasn't through being told. Maybe it would make up for the news of her disappearance being shuffled away so long ago.

One thing bothered me about the search for Honey's killer: If Gabe Davis didn't kill her, and Bobby Johnson didn't kill her, then who did?

19

It's a beautiful article." I tried not to get any tears on the newspaper. Travis Bush had done better than I'd expected. Momma agreed to talk to him about Jewel, and I think it did her some good that someone besides family wanted to know about her. Not that she was in any hurry to find Bobby. The idea that Jewel's story was told at last brought Momma some comfort, I think.

Ben handed me a tissue. A beautiful Saturday morning, and a rare occasion with Ben not working. We slept in like newlyweds, ate breakfast in bed. Labor Day was coming, and before that, Di and Steve's move to Jackson.

In a few hours I'd head to her place to help her with her yard sale. But this time was just for Ben and me.

"I wonder if Momma bought enough copies to give to the family." I scanned one of the paragraphs. "*Thirty years ago, a bank robbery. And the bank bags finally turned up, confirming what the Kincaids had suspected all along: Jewel Kincaid did not leave Greenburg without a word to her beloved family. Instead, she lay buried in a field for those three decades, and some of the stolen money remained tucked inside her suitcase, hidden in a junk shop. Then, several weeks ago, Honey Haggerty was murdered in her restaurant. Her alleged killer waits in County Jail for his arraignment. Here's where you come in. The Greenburg Police Department is seeking a mutual friend of Honey's and Jewel's, a Mr. Robert Johnson, known as Bobby.*

They believe he has information vital to both cases. And then it ends with a plea if anyone knows of Bobby's whereabouts, to contact the Greenburg PD."

"I wonder if they've gotten any calls yet." Ben yawned and stretched. "So this is what sleeping in feels like."

"Makes me feel lazy, too. Why did I ever get into retail? Don't get me wrong. I love making soap. The scents, getting the temperatures right. Did you know, lavender really is soothing?" A mew sounded by my feet. Spot, offended that Ben's stretching had disrupted her morning nap. "But the hours. So many things come up and I have to close. I'm grateful for the Internet orders."

"You can always close on weekends. Or stay open half a day on Saturdays. Or hire someone else part-time with Sadie heading back to Nashville. Or better yet, expand your Web store and change to strictly online shopping."

"I could do that." Scaling back the store wasn't like quitting. Or was it? I reached for another drink of my coffee.

"Plus, once we start a family, you'll want to be able to get away more easily."

"True."

Suddenly I had the fidgets. I wasn't due at Di's house for two more hours. Shapers. That's where I'd go. I needed to work out and think.

Ben was attempting to read the paper but kept nodding and blinking away sleep. "What? Where are you going?"

I found some clean shorts and a T-shirt. "Shapers.

I need to get in a workout before I go to Di's and sit around for the afternoon. Get in better shape."

"Your *shape* looks fine to me."

"Very cute." I tossed my nightshirt in the laundry basket. "Gravity has more of an effect once a woman hits thirty-five."

"Go ahead and have your workout. Just gravitate to me before you leave, darlin'."

———

The Saturday streets of Greenburg seemed less crowded than usual. Everyone else was probably sleeping in, too. When I entered Shapers, Vivian Delane waited behind the reception desk, leaning on the counter and drawing on a note pad. The customary peppy music wasn't playing through the speakers. A fluorescent light buzzed somewhere.

Vivian's normally flawless complexion didn't have its usual texture today. Another crisis must have presented itself. I immediately scolded myself for the thought. She needed a listening ear and didn't deserve my disdain. How many times had I gone out without make-up because of being preoccupied with something else? Especially after the kitchen tile war, as Ben and I called it when we haggled back and forth on which shade of ceramic to install.

"Good morning." I shifted my exercise bag from my shoulder. "Thought I'd stop by for a quick round on the machines. Maybe try some of that kickboxing, too."

Her whisper of a smile didn't reach her sad eyes.

"You're the first one who's come in today. I probably shouldn't have opened, but I know routines help us when we're going through tough times." She glanced away from me.

"What's wrong? Is it Curtis again?" I touched her arm.

Vivian nodded. A tear streaked down her cheek. "We. . .we had a big fight. It's over. He left me."

As she straightened to her full height, something shiny near her throat caught the reflected sunlight outside and made me blink—a golden heart locket with a filigree engraving on its front.

"What a beautiful necklace." I tried not to gulp for air. "Is that vintage?" Part of me knew there were probably hundreds, if not thousands, of heart lockets with filigree swirls on the front, just like Aunt Jewel's. Part of me wondered at another possibility. Yeah, right. Like I'd call Jerry every time I saw a golden locket. It's like when you get a new car, and you start noticing everyone else who drives the same model and the same color.

Vivian nodded and ran a finger over the golden heart. "I usually don't wear jewelry this dainty to the gym. I'm always afraid I'll break it."

"Where. . .where did you get it, if you don't mind me asking?"

"Curtis bought it from an antiques shop. I'd seen it at a shop over in Adamsville. So he went back, got it for me, and surprised me."

"Oh. Does it open?"

"It's stuck, so I've never tried to find out," Vivian admitted. "I didn't want to break the hinges or anything."

"Sorry, didn't mean to sound nosy." I licked my lips. "My aunt who, um, passed away years ago had one like it. I actually wouldn't mind finding a similar one for my mom." Which I actually hadn't decided until now. At least it sounded like a good idea.

"There's probably a lot of necklaces in little stores in these backwoods towns around here. The store in Adamsville is called Vintage Treasures." Vivian moved to the wall calendar and erased some class schedules.

"Good idea." I ignored her crack about backwoods towns and toted my bag to the first machine. Hurt people hurt people, so the saying goes. "Do you mind if I just drag my bag around with me? I'm not planning to stay long."

"Go right ahead."

I started with the warm-up machine, a gentle stair-stepper. "So, do you think Curtis will come back? Is there a chance?"

Vivian sank back onto her stool at the desk. "I don't know. Would you believe, for the first time in twenty years, I don't know what to do? This isn't my town. I never wanted to come here. No offense."

"Is there someone you can talk to? A minister?"

"No preacher could help us."

"God can fix your marriage. I know I'm new to being married, but I've heard of other couples who've come back from the brink of divorce. After infidelity, addiction." Already I could feel my muscles getting stronger as I worked along the circuit.

"I'm not into anything like that. But thanks for the suggestion, anyway." She smiled at me as if I were a child proposing to mop up a dirty kitchen floor with one paper towel. "If you need anything, holler. I'll be in the back." With a whirl, Vivian retreated to the office where Curtis usually holed up.

I forced my attention back to the machines and battling my body into submission. So I probably hadn't taken the best approach with Vivian. I'd tried. Maybe someone else could help her one day.

Of course, someone could tell us the truth all day long and if we didn't believe it, there was nothing the other person could do. Or we could even know the truth ourselves but still not be convinced of it all the way down to our souls. The whole motherhood thing, for example. I dashed some sweat from my forehead.

People could tell me what a great mom I'd be, how it's always different when they're "your kids." Even the other day talking to Di at the bank about her experiences being a mother still couldn't convince me until *I* was ready. The same thing about a person's reliance on God, or lack thereof.

One thing I did know, I had family praying for me. Not so much that I'd "see the light" and have a child. But more that I'd realize I didn't have to repeat the mistakes of the family before me, that like it or not, my little future angelic children would get minds of their own and test their limits, and that free will stretches a long way. And God's grace stretches even farther.

I'd almost made the circuit around to the beginning, just like my thoughts came around full circle and brought me back to Vivian's situation. How could I share with her the very thing I struggled with myself: believing that God wanted to take care of us in our frailty. Maybe I couldn't get past the times it seemed like He'd failed me. But I *knew* He never failed us or looked the other way. Yet Aunt Jewel still ended up in an early grave. I made myself stop that line of thought. Just like I'd "seen" Aunt Jewel in my dream, so God had seen her make poor choices, and let her make them. Free will. A double-edged sword. Faith in His love tempers the blade, but my human self still hurt.

My arms throbbed from the biceps and triceps machines. I was more than reaping the consequences of my free will in the past by slacking off on workouts. This afternoon I'd be no use to Di except to lounge around on her porch and drink tea. Maybe I could haggle with yard sale customers, but that bordered too much on retail activity for my day off. Still, I'd treasure the time spent with her. And I'd wonder how many people had called the newspaper about Bobby Johnson.

20

By Tuesday morning Greenburg had embraced its latest fad. Someone had started distributing buttons that proclaimed *I SAW BOBBY JOHNSON* in red, white, and blue. I was walking down the sidewalk toward the post office when I saw one for the first time.

"Where did you get that button?" I asked the gray-haired man so loudly that it startled him.

His hearing aid squealed, and he adjusted it. "Some kid was selling them down near the town square. A dollar. It's a fund-raiser."

"A fund-raiser?"

"Supposedly to help pay for burying the girl found in that field."

I quickened my pace. I was going to hurt Travis Bush, and I would be put in jail for it. Ben would hear about it on the news, and so would Di, all the way up in Jackson. My heart ached. Di and Steve's moving van had already come and gone, and they were spending the kids' last week of summer vacation in their new home. I figured I ought to take it out on someone.

There he was, the young blond story-hunter, strolling around downtown, schmoozing as if he were running for office. When he saw me, a big grin spread across his dimpled face.

"Mrs. Hartley! Isn't this great?" He looked like someone had held him down and pinned red, white, and blue buttons all over the front of his shirt.

"Travis. What are you doing?"

"I'm helping *you* find Bobby Johnson." Travis unpinned a button from his shirt and held it out to me. "Here. Your button is free. Grandma Fleta filled me in more after I talked to your mother. I think a Memphis or Nashville television might be picking up the story. A producer called the *Dispatch* this morning."

"You don't say." I held the pin like it might bite me. "A man told me something about this being a fund-raiser?" If this was a scam of any kind. . .

"After I wrote your mother's article, I started thinking." At this, his face grew serious. "Your mother's family had no insurance for her sister's burial. And it's the least we can do around here to pitch in. Hopefully by creating a buzz about Bobby, people's memories will be jogged. Especially the forty-five-and-older crowd. Think of it as Greenburg's Most Wanted."

"Don't you realize what you're doing?" I stuffed the button in my purse.

"You're not going to wear your button?"

"Yes. No. But this might drive Bobby into hiding. Maybe he'll leave and then we'll never hear from him again."

Someone drove by, horn honking. "I saw Bobby Johnson! Whoo-eee!"

"This is making a mockery of our story." Momma was going to have a fit, and I'd hear about the whole thing when she called me. She probably thought she would gain some closure, and maybe help someone else who'd lost a loved one like she'd lost Aunt Jewel, but this. . .this sideshow?

A couple was leaving City Hall and approached us. "What are those buttons for? Is someone running for office?"

"No. We're looking for a missing man, gone for thirty years." Travis whipped out a brochure. "And here's the story of a long-lost love."

"Oh, how sad," the wife murmured as she scanned the page. She tugged on her husband's sleeve. "Honey, let's donate something to that poor girl's family."

After the couple moved on to their car, I looked at Travis. "Don't you need a permit or something like that to sell anything, even for a fund-raiser?"

"Got it right here." Travis slapped his back pocket.

"Unbelievable."

"Scoff all you want. The newspaper has already received over a dozen calls. Look out, guys forty-nine to fifty-three. If you're really Bobby Johnson with secrets to hide, I'm going to find you. And then the law will want to talk to you. I'm passing everything on to Officer Hartley."

"But I know Bobby won't talk to you."

"Why not?"

"Because he already talked to me." I crossed my arms in front of me. "One night he responded to that ad I put in the newspaper. We talked, briefly. He's a sad man. I just want him to stop running for his own peace, and my family's. I know Greenburg PD is working to find him, too."

"Can I quote you on that?"

"Quote all you want." I watched as Travis sold another button. "I have to go open my business."

After I picked up my mail and my stamps, of course. I headed into the Greenburg post office and saw Roland Thacker at his mailbox. He looked like a leftover thundercloud.

Roland slammed the little mailbox door then turned his glare on me. "Are you responsible for that one-man media circus outside?"

"No, I'm not." I moved a few steps down to the mailbox for Tennessee River Soaps and almost felt like slamming the door myself. "I think it's going to do more harm than good."

"I'm going to hold you responsible if my name ends up getting dragged into this mess." Roland pointed at me.

"He took the story and made it bigger. They're looking for a man who disappeared a long time ago." I pulled out a stack of bills and a few catalogs.

"If he's not careful, he'll end up dragging out more than just Bobby's story." With that, Roland stalked off toward the front door.

After almost a week of the "I saw Bobby Johnson" ruckus, Ben and I made an executive decision, took the weekend off, and fled to Jackson. I made sure I called Momma on our way home again to Greenburg.

Understandably, Momma still had strong opinions about the Bobby Johnson buttons. "Would you believe the nerve of people? No respect for the dead, I tell ya." Her anger crackled across the phone line. "I know they said they're helping pay her funeral bill, but. . ."

I'd already checked my voicemail and there was no news from Travis Bush. "But maybe someone will believe us that there really *is* a Bobby Johnson around Greenburg and actually help us find him."

"I don't know if that'll work. Maybe I shouldn't have talked to that reporter." Momma heaved a sigh. "Are you on your way home yet?"

"Yes, Momma." I smiled across the cab of the pickup truck at Ben. "We left Jackson half an hour ago. You're going to love Di and Steve's house."

"I'd love it if it were closer."

"I know. But now when we want to get out of town, we have somewhere to go."

"Now, what would I want to get out of town for?" Momma clicked her tongue. "Your daddy and I are going up to visit them on Labor Day weekend. One of the boys said something about a train museum."

"That's right. They have a Casey Jones museum. We could hardly get Taylor to leave with all the trains." I smiled at the memory.

"Sounds like you're practicin' for some kids."

"Maybe." I didn't want to talk about that at the moment.

"Call me when you get home."

"I sure will, Momma." I glanced up as we ended the call. Ben and I were approaching the sign for Leisure Lodge. "Honey, let's stop and say hi to Papaw. I told him I'd bring you the next time I came."

Ben drove into the parking lot and acted like he didn't want to get out of the truck. "All righty then."

"It's not so bad. Just think of Papaw and how

happy he'll be to see us." With this latest development of attacking visitors, I wondered if they'd moved Papaw to a more secure unit. We started crossing toward the main doors of the home. Ben hung back.

"Baby, are you okay?" I slowed my pace.

He reached for my hand. "It's just hard comin' here. Every Sunday when I was a kid, my parents would drag me to visit my grandparents. Not a fun place to visit. I'll try, but it's hard."

"We won't stay long. I keep thinkin', the whole time I'm here, that I'm doing it for Papaw. To make his day happier. It's not about me."

Ben pulled the handle on one of the large wooden doors to the home. "I'll try."

We headed for the reception desk. I found out Papaw was still in the same room. Today he reclined on his bed and had his newspapers spread out over his lap.

"Andi-girl, you came back." He smiled, and I saw the Papaw I'd remembered as a child. "And you brought your Ben, too."

"I said I would."

Ben dragged an extra chair to Papaw's end of the room. "So, how are you, Mr. Kincaid?"

"Fair to middlin'." Papaw's smile left. "They doped me up some more. Stupid doctors. But I know what I saw. Bobby Johnson in the flesh, walkin' down the hallway."

"Are you sure? It's been a long time since you've seen him. People change over the years." I glanced at Ben, who was reading one of Papaw's scandal papers with the headline, "FROZEN ALIENS FOUND IN THE ALPS."

"Put forty pounds on him and a bunch of pomade on that hair of his, but it's still him under all that tryin' to look like someone famous." Papaw tossed the paper he'd been reading and picked up another one. "The dummies can't see what's under their noses."

"Momma was really worried about you the other day. Papaw, you just can't go around hitting people."

"Stop talkin' to me like I'm a five-year-old. He made me so mad, I couldn't help myself."

I changed the subject to Diana and Steve's move and how we'd all get to see Papaw more now that we'd be going back and forth to Jackson. He would look at Ben, then at me, and then at his papers. Momma must have brought them.

When the first snore came from Papaw's mouth, I whispered to Ben, "I guess we can go now." Ben nodded and closed the magazine he'd been reading.

Papaw opened one of his eyes. "You leavin' me again?"

"I'll be back. Promise."

"Love ya, Andi-girl."

I gave him one last wave before Ben and I headed back to the reception desk. The three-ring binder lay right where I'd left it when I signed us in. Other visitors had come and gone, signing in and signing out.

"Ben." A thought struck me. What if Bobby Johnson really *had* visited the nursing home? And Papaw had really seen him? I started turning pages to find any Johnsons listed on the visitors' record. The nurse at the desk barely glanced at me and kept talking on the phone.

Several Johnsons. Sophie Johnson, visited by Judy

Kane. Rufus Johnson, visited by Wayne Johnson. Then I found another name.

"Pay dirt."

Edna Johnson had been visited by Curtis Delane, this very afternoon. *Looking like someone famous. Brent Balducci, huh?*

"What do we do now?" Ben gunned the engine as we shot down the road back toward Greenburg.

"I'm calling Jerry. He needs to know about Curtis visiting Edna Johnson." Rows of tall pines flashed by the truck. "I just talked to Vivian on Saturday morning. I wonder if Curtis ever came home again."

All I got was the ever-efficient Fleta at the dispatch desk. Remembering who her grandson was, I only left Jerry a message, asking him to call us and that it was urgent. A call to Jerry's cell phone went straight to voicemail. I explained as briefly as I could about Curtis/Bobby then hung up.

"You were right about the alias," Ben admitted.

"But why'd he come back? What would be the point, if he knew he might get caught?"

"Remember where we came from? Edna Johnson. The lady who owned the egg farm." Ben shook his head. "Curtis wanted to be closer to his momma. And he dragged Vivian to Greenburg right along with him."

"Vivian said he'd left her. So he's got to be in the area somewhere if he's still visiting his mother."

Clouds rolled in from the west. A welcome late

summer storm would descend on us soon. I glanced to the side of the road, where an exit for a rest stop merged off the highway. A familiar figure was walking from the covered patio. Curtis.

"Ben. . .there he is. . ." My throat constricted. "We need to go back around and talk to him."

"What are we going to say, exactly? Beg him to turn himself in?" Ben slowed the truck and got off at the next exit, circled around through the underpass, and got us going back toward the rest stop.

"I don't know. Talk to him. Maybe he *will* turn himself in. Or we can at least stall him until Jerry can get here or send someone. I'll figure something out."

"That doesn't give me much confidence."

In five minutes we were pulling off at the rest stop. My stomach sort of growled anyway. Maybe they had snack machines or something.

Curtis's car still remained parked in the lot when we pulled into a nearby space. I glanced inside the passenger window of his average-looking blue sedan. Candy wrappers and fast food boxes littered the front seat. A pillow and blanket covered part of the backseat. So he'd left Vivian but hadn't gone far. He couldn't use credit cards if someone decided to look for him. The rest stop was a short trip to Leisure Lodge.

A van roared off the highway and parked near the covered patio. A family streamed out like a line of circus clowns climbing from a miniature car. The first drops of rain splattered the pavement then turned into a downpour before Ben and I reached the covered walkway to the rest rooms. Two rows of vending machines faced each other, sodas on one side and snacks on the other.

Curtis stood at a snack machine. He stiffened when he saw us. "Andromeda. Ben."

"Um, hello. What are you doing here?" I asked.

"Same as you. Stopping and resting." He chuckled. I failed to see what Aunt Jewel had seen in him. His left cheek had a faded bruise. From Papaw's attack, maybe? Normally he wore neatly pressed cotton button-down shirts. This one looked like he'd slept in it for a few days. What happened to the romantic guitar player who wanted to run away and get married, only to get ensnared in a bank robbery? Or was the desire to make something of himself stronger than his love for Aunt Jewel? Children's squeals echoed off the bathroom walls inside. Someone turned on a sink. More squeals.

"We just left Leisure Lodge. My Papaw's there. I try to see him when I can. But it's hard, running a business." I studied the snack machine. "Ben, did you want a snack?"

"Sure. I'll get us some sodas." Ben moved to the drink machines. With him around, I knew Curtis wouldn't hurt me. Not that there was any danger. I thought of Aunt Jewel once more.

"That's good of you to visit him." Curtis popped the top of a can of soda. "Lots of older people get forgotten."

"Papaw has Alzheimer's, you know." A package of Ho-Hos seemed to wave at me from inside one of the machines. No, I'd buy the small bag of peanuts and share it with Ben. "Some days it's like he's living in another decade. Sees people who've been gone for years. He even called me Jewel one time. Funny, because I don't look a thing like her."

"Alzheimer's is a hard disease to face. My mother has terminal cancer. It's not long for her now. But I'm glad she's not alone." Curtis glanced at the family who came out of each set of rest rooms. Now they commenced squealing and bickering over the sodas.

Ben got out of their way just in time and rejoined us. "Here. I got you the diet."

"Thanks." I found a dollar bill in my shorts pocket and fed it to the machine then selected the bag of peanuts. "Curtis, I've taken your wife's advice and used exercise as a way to help cope with stress."

The family bustled their way from the rest stop courtyard and moved toward their van. My phone warbled. *Jerry.* I passed the phone to Ben, who took it and stepped over toward the soda machines.

"As a matter of fact, I saw Vivian a week ago Saturday, and she told me—"

"What did she tell you?" He stepped closer.

"That you, um, left her." I glanced around the covered courtyard. "Have you been staying here? At the rest stop? Why not at a hotel? Or with friends?"

"I can't afford a hotel. And I really don't have friends around here. At least not ones who'd take me in." Curtis shrugged and headed a few steps toward the outside parking area. Ben moved to block his path.

"I know you went to see Edna on Saturday," I called after Curtis. "She's your mother, isn't she?"

Curtis broke into a run.

21

We dashed into the downpour after Curtis. He'd already jumped into his car and thrown it into reverse. Its back end fishtailed as he accelerated. Ben's truck with its well-tuned V8 engine would keep up easily. He turned the key, and the engine roared to life.

"Follow him!" I strained to see through the rain-blurry windshield at the road leading onto the highway.

"That's what I'm trying to do. Jerry's on his way." Ben hit reverse, and we slid backwards onto the access road. Curtis's nondescript sedan was merging onto the main road, free of traffic.

He took the road to Greenburg and Ben's truck matched him mile for mile. The windshield wipers did their job.

"Jerry's going to try to head us off at the bridge. Or at least look for Curtis."

"Is he going to meet us in time?"

The sedan darted into the left lane and passed a slow-moving delivery truck. Ben's knuckles whitened on the steering wheel. "He's going to hydroplane if he doesn't slow down. Hang on. That other truck's pulling over."

We shot past the delivery truck. All I could do was hold back the tears and hang onto the armrest. "I hope Jerry makes it to the bridge in time."

This was my fault. I had only wanted to talk to Curtis and encourage him to go talk to Jerry. And my big mouth had driven him to flee. I didn't need to cry.

The rain streaking along the side windows of the truck was enough.

And poor Momma. She'd shared from her heart with Travis Bush to let him tell her story. I'd hoped if Bobby read the article, he'd do the right thing and cooperate with the police. Evidently his thirty-year habit of running wouldn't die easily.

Here came the Greenburg city limits sign.

Curtis approached the Tennessee River bridge. At the midpoint of the concrete and steel structure, his sedan jerked wildly then slammed into the guardrail. I cupped my hand over my mouth and stifled my scream. Then Curtis's car skidded across the other lanes of traffic and slammed into the opposite railing.

"Ben, pull over!"

Our truck moved to the shoulder and Ben shifted into park. Thankfully, the rain had prevented much traffic—not many people wanted to venture out this afternoon. A solitary car crested the bridge and paused.

Ben lowered his window.

The other vehicle's window glided down, and the driver waved at us. "I've just called 911, but I can't stay."

"We'll be here," Ben said. I nodded. The other car moved on to the other side of the river.

Ben and I darted across to the opposite side of the roadway. Curtis was leaving his car. He staggered to the side of the bridge. The side panels and fenders of his car looked like crumpled tin.

"Bobby. . .Curtis, please wait." I reached him first.

The rain soaked our hair, our clothes, and oil patches on the road pooled on the water-soaked concrete. Ben moved to the rear of his car, now facing the Greenburg side of the river.

"I don't have to say anything to you." Rain dripped from the ends of his hair and drizzled onto his neck.

"I know you didn't mean it. I know you loved her. And it was a long time ago. You said as much the other night." The rain made me shiver.

Another vehicle slowed, but Ben waved them on. He glanced toward the end of the bridge, and back at me. He mouthed "Jerry" when I looked past Curtis in Ben's direction. Ben started walking toward the squad car that I assume waited at the other end of the bridge. Sirens wailed.

"I'll still go to prison. . . ." Curtis turned to face the concrete railing and the roaring Tennessee River below. No longer at flood stage, but definitely not safe for tubing on a lazy afternoon or taking a swim.

"Did you get much of the money from that robbery?"

Curtis whirled in my direction.

"We found the bank bags in the back room of Honey's office. And I imagine that packet of bills I found in my aunt Jewel's suitcase will be identified as some of the ones missing in that robbery."

He slumped against the guardrail. "I only wanted some money to help us get away."

"Bobby. I don't fault you wantin' some money. But people usually *earn* it."

"Jewel and I were goin' to get married. But then

Jewel figured out about the robbery Honey and I pulled off. Honey didn't want me to tell her, and for that she was going to give us a ride to Memphis. Somehow Jewel knew. She was smart. Smart like you."

"Why did you come back?"

"My mother. I told you earlier that she doesn't have long now. A little over a year ago, the doctor said she had eighteen months. I didn't want her to leave this world feeling alone and never knowing about me."

"I can understand that."

"Your aunt would've been proud of you." Curtis, whom I still struggled to think of as Bobby, quirked a hint of a smile. "You were such a little thing when I left. We took you to the park once. Do you remember?"

I shook my head.

"And fishing. One pretty summer day, hot enough to fry eggs on the pavement. Everything your aunt Jewel did, you wanted to do, too. She would've made a great mother." I wasn't sure, but I thought I saw a few tears mingle with the rain on Bobby's cheeks.

"I do remember the fishing. The sun sparkled on the river, and Aunt Jewel's hair looked like gold. I remember that I wished mine did."

A sudden movement made us look toward town. Jerry approached in his squad car, with only the headlights lit. Another car blocked the other side of the road. Jerry stopped the vehicle and got out to join us.

"Curtis Delane. Bobby Johnson." Jerry strode in our direction. "We need to talk."

Curtis glanced at me, then at Jerry. "I'm not going to jail."

"That's not for us to decide. But I have some questions about the night of Harriet Haggerty's murder."

"I was at home with Vivian after the Chamber of Commerce meeting. Besides, don't you already have a suspect in custody awaiting arraignment?"

Jerry shrugged. "We do. But when new information comes to light, we must reevaluate our course of action. So says the DA. Bobby Johnson, we have a lot of questions for you."

"I don't know what you're talking about with this 'Bobby Johnson.'" Curtis looked Jerry straight in the eye.

I shivered again. I couldn't make my feet move, but if I drew attention to myself Jerry just might order me to leave.

Jerry seemed intent on giving Bobby a long, even look in return. "Don't give me that. It won't take long, but we can verify you're Robert Johnson. You can only run for so long."

"I didn't kill Honey." Bobby's chuckle sounded nervous. "I might have wanted to strangle her a few times when we were younger. Bad choice of words, but that was Honey. Back then, I considered her a good friend."

"Tell me something I don't know." Jerry crossed his arms in front of his chest.

"Bobby, I do know you loved my aunt Jewel." I hoped Jerry didn't mind me talking. An ambulance rolled up and stopped near Jerry's car. "What happened was a crime of passion. But I want to know. . .was Honey blackmailing you?"

"She figured out who I was. Gave me instructions

about where to come and when to bring the money. Thought I was still rich or something." Bobby placed one hand on the metal railing atop the concrete. "But I didn't kill her."

"We don't have to talk here," Jerry said. "It's pourin' rain, and your car's wrecked. A tow truck is on the way, and we need to get traffic moving. We can chat in my office."

"I didn't kill Honey." Bobby ventured another look over the side of the bridge. "And I'm not about to let you take me for *that*."

In slow motion, Bobby grabbed the metal railing. Jerry and I both ran for him, but Bobby swung his legs over the side like a gymnast on a pommel horse. Gravity took over. Then came a splash.

I screamed. Jerry shouted. We leaned over the railing and scanned the rushing water fifty feet below. Bobby, a dark blob below us, drifted on the current. He looked up at me and gave the same salute I'd seen at the cemetery the day of Aunt Jewel's memorial. Jerry hit the button on his two-way radio, hollering for dispatch to call the other counties downstream and alert them of Bobby's escape.

"We'll talk later, Andi." Jerry ran for his car.

I ran for Ben.

———

They never found a body, not after days of searching. A hiker found Bobby's shirt near the riverbank, so the authorities didn't rule out the idea that Bobby had survived and moved on again. I wondered if he would try to contact Vivian. The police probably did, too. I stopped by Shapers three days after Bobby jumped, only to find the ladies' gym closed. It was probably just as well. Ben had mentioned at breakfast about joining a gym in Savannah, and we could get a couple's discount. Another thing we could do together.

The first weekend in September came, and with it the last watermelons from our field. This fall, before the first frost, Ben and I would have the field plowed under, something that should have been done long ago.

Ben carried a watermelon to our covered patio and laid it on the picnic table. "Last one." He gave me a little-boy grin of triumph.

"Yes, it is." I touched the watermelon. "I don't want to plant watermelons. Not like we ever have. Honey, I assume, planted them year after year. With us workin' on the house, I hadn't even thought about a garden. But I want something different to grow in the field next year."

"What do you want to plant?" Ben took me in his arms.

"Tomatoes. Lettuce. Carrots. Everything for a good salad. Maybe some fruit trees." I wrapped my arms around him. "And cucumbers. I'd love to learn to make pickles. Squash, too."

"Aren't you the ambitious one? One afternoon of making pickled watermelon rind with your momma, and you're a canning expert?"

"Let's just say I learned a new skill. And after everything we've been through, I also learned one more thing. God gives us all a choice. Jewel, Bobby, even my nephews who are drivin' their own momma crazy. And one day, when we're a momma and a daddy, we'll do the best we can. And no less. What they do is eventually up to them." Once I finished that speech, all I did was smile at Ben.

"You mean. . . ?"

I nodded. "I want you to be a daddy."

Ben gave a whoop, picked me up, and spun me around then set me back down. He pulled me back into his arms and leaned closer to kiss me.

The sound of a vehicle roaring up the driveway made us pause and turn. A red, white, and blue delivery van stopped behind Ben's truck. Out hopped a driver with a flat envelope.

"Good afternoon." He nodded at Ben, then me. "Andromeda Clark?"

"That's me. Before I was married, anyway."

"Sign right here." The courier handed me an electronic signature pad and the envelope.

Before the sounds of the delivery van had vanished, I had the envelope open. A folded white piece of paper was inside.

"Who's it from?"

"I'm not sure." The postmark on the envelope read Muscle Shoals, Alabama. I sat down at the picnic table and unfolded the paper. Three sentences. *Her locket was taken from me. I'm sorry, but I couldn't get it back before I left. Be well.*

22

I was cooking, and I was humming. This was remarkable because normally cooking for me involved muttering and throwing things in the trash can, and bad smells. Our kitchen table brimmed with sliced watermelon, zipper baggies of rind, and a bowl in front of me where I placed peeled rind. Momma had given me her recipe, and for once, I wasn't going to call her or anyone else for help. Then I'd proudly show everyone a neat box of jars full of pickled watermelon rind. Maybe I'd have enough to take to the farmers market. Spare pocket money would come in handy. Or they'd make great Christmas gifts—just add a bow and a coordinating bar of soap.

Vivian had held a memorial service for Curtis. When she spoke to the crowd at First Community Church, she told us that Curtis deserved to be remembered, that no one had known or truly understood what he'd gone through in his life. Although the police had told her about and even shown her the shirt they'd found, she refused to believe he had survived the river. It seemed as though once she'd lost him, she intended to keep him away from her life.

Jerry shook his head as he stood next to Ben and me. "Even after you gave me that envelope, she still doesn't believe Curtis is alive. She told me she 'could feel that he was lost to her forever.' Why would she want him gone if she loved him so much?"

"I don't understand," I told Jerry then. "Do you think he'll ever be caught?"

"One day. Even if he escapes the authorities. We all pay one way or another."

Today, three days later, I felt like I needed to do something productive. Between shivers of excitement at the thought of starting a family, and the hurt of what had been done to mine, I didn't know whether to rejoice or cry. Aunt Jewel had been a star in the darkness, extinguished too quickly.

I sliced the rind into perfect chunks, just like Momma would have done. Aunt Jewel would have chopped haphazardly, with abandon. But she didn't abandon her family. Now that we all knew this, I think it gave Momma a measure of peace.

The ringing phone made me jump. I put the knife on the cutting board.

It was Vivian Delane, or Johnson, rather. "Andi, hi. Um, are you up for some company?"

"Sure. I'm just doing some stuff in the kitchen. Come on by. I just made some iced tea." She'd never come to the house before. I wasn't quite sure if it was a pleasant surprise for me or not. So I decided to brace myself for her conversation spiced with an occasional acerbic comment.

"Is Ben there? I mean, I don't want to be a bother, with you two being newlyweds and all. . ."

"You're not a bother. Ben's at the restaurant. Where else would he be?"

"Okay, then. I'll be there soon."

Vivian arrived within five minutes. She must not

have been too far away. "Thanks. You have a cute place."
She scanned the kitchen, then ambled to the nearest
chair that didn't have watermelon rind blocking it.

"So how are you doing? Have you decided what
you're going to do yet?" I had so many questions I
wanted to ask her about Bobby. When did she guess at
his double life? What about his secrets? Instead, I kept
my mouth shut and poured her a glass of tea, plus one
for myself. "Lemon?"

"Please. I love lemon. It's good for digestion."

Once I sliced her some lemon, she squeezed some
into her tea and stirred then took a sip. "Delicious."
She took another sip, but her hand shook as she held
the glass.

"I'm leaving town. Trudy at the coffee shop has
bought Shapers from me. Once that deal's tied up, I'll
be free of this place. I wanted to say good-bye. You
were one of our best regulars." A tear slid down her
cheek. "I loved Curtis so much. I'd have done anything
for him. But he picks here, of all places, to come back
to. I thought my love was enough. Guess not."

"He must have been tormented, to have carried
his secret for so long." Try as I might, I hadn't been able
to get angry at Curtis/Bobby. All I wanted to do was
weep over what had been lost. Greed had killed Jewel,
not just Bobby's crime of passion. But today wasn't a
day to cry. Today was for me to learn and grow, even
if it was just making pickled watermelon rind. Aunt
Jewel would have liked that.

"Truly, I never figured his secret out. Not for
years." Vivian stared out toward the side yard.

"What do you mean?" I started slicing again. Nice, even chunks. My mouth watered at the thought of the rind. Summer in a jar.

"It was the locket." Vivian reached into her pocket and set a gold heart locket and chain on the table. "I found it one day, hidden, and when I asked Curtis about it, he said it was a birthday gift. He acted bashful as a little boy at it being found. And I loved it. I could tell it was old. Then I opened it up. Saw your parents' pictures inside. A picture of a little girl. You, I assume. He'd never opened it. When I asked him about it, he told me he'd gotten it in an antique store. Then we moved to Greenburg, and I started some checking around on my own."

"Thank you for giving this to me." My voice caught in my throat. "I'll make sure my momma gets the locket. She'll treasure it." But Vivian had known it was Aunt Jewel's that first day when I commented on the locket at Shapers. And she hadn't said anything. She'd lied when I'd asked her about it, too. That hurt. And now I'd received that cryptic note from Bobby. Not a coincidence. I didn't understand why she felt she needed to lie and say that Bobby had given her the locket. Bobby might have killed Aunt Jewel, but my heart told me he'd been truthful with me.

"So you see why I have to go." She touched a bag of rinds, then pulled her hand back as if she'd touched a hot stove. "Too much sadness has happened in this town. Poor Honey, someone choking her with that watermelon rind. Then Curtis. . .what he did to your aunt. I wished he'd have told me himself. Might have been easier for everyone all around."

I wanted to remind her of all the beautiful and joyful things in Greenburg; about fishing on the river, or tubing. Our annual fireworks display and the Christmas light decorating contest. And although sometimes we got things wrong, some of us still strived to make things right. But I couldn't this time.

The counter shifted in front of me, and it wasn't because of an earthquake or a sinkhole under the house.

Poor Honey, someone choking her with that watermelon rind. . .

The *Dispatch* and the television news had never been that specific. Rumor and speculation had circulated about strangulation. But no one had ever mentioned the watermelon rinds.

Only Jerry knew, plus Ben and me.

And Honey's killer.

While Vivian wept quietly and drank her tea, I tried to figure out what to do. My cell phone was inches away on the counter. What if I called someone? And what if I was wrong and was making an assumption? I'd been wrong about Roland paying Honey blackmail money. Being wrong this time would cause needless pain and embarrassment to a grieving woman.

"How did you know that?" I shouldn't have opened my mouth. I should have made an excuse to leave the room and call Jerry or Ben or someone. I could have been discreet. But I had to open my mouth. My hand gripped the knife. If she thought about jumping me, maybe she'd think again if she saw I held a knife. And maybe I was crazy. The knife split the last bit of rind on the cutting board.

"What are you talking about?" Her voice shook.

"Vivian." I turned and faced her, relaxing my grip on the knife. "Did you go out to the restaurant that night, trying to talk some sense into her? Was she the one you thought Bobby was running off to see?"

"I'm leaving town. Too much has happened. Curtis knew I'd do anything for him." Vivian stood. "Anything to make her leave us alone, quit bleeding our account every month. Those meetings at night. At this stupid field of all places. He said Honey told him it was far enough from town and served as a good reminder of what they'd both had to live with."

My lungs felt like I was trying to breathe through a straw. "We can talk to Jerry, get this sorted out. Before you leave town, of course." As if he'd let her leave. But I had to get her calm. She looked like a caged animal, starting to pace. The phone lay on the counter, inches from where I worked.

Vivian came at me like a leopard. My head struck the edge of the sink. White-hot pain. Hands around my throat.

Not like Honey. I reached for her eyes, the world blackening around me. *Jesus. Help me.* I scratched. Heard her scream.

It was enough for her to loosen her grip. Now the room spun. I staggered to my feet. Viselike hands grabbed one of my legs from below, but not before I snatched my phone from the counter.

I kicked in her direction then slipped on a piece of rind on the floor.

Vivian was on me again, pulling on my neck. Again I scratched, tried to land another kick. *Please work, phone.*

I had Ben on speed dial. Pushed the number with the thumb of my free hand. Pushed the phone away from us. It slid across the floor as it dialed.

"Oh, no you don't!" Vivian released her hold on me and sprang for the phone.

It was my turn to give chase. "Ben! Help me!" I leapt for Vivian and tackled her. Stevie and his junior league football team would be proud.

A tile floor hurts when you land on it. Hard. The air left Vivian's lungs—and mine—at the same time. I tried to scream but could only cough while Vivian struggled to reach the phone. She reminded me of the time I'd chased a greased pig when I was a kid.

Finally, I managed to scream.

"Shut up!" Vivian kicked at me, but I rolled and she missed.

"No. You give up, Vivian. Ben's going to call the police, and they'll be here in five minutes. Talk to Jerry. You can get a good lawyer."

"You should have kept quiet." Vivian stood, panting. Her cheek had a few scratches from my fingernails. She moved toward me again.

"I know. But I wanted to be wrong about you, Vivian." I backpedaled and bumped into the counter. Felt Momma's old ceramic bowl behind me.

I grabbed it, watermelon rind flying, and pegged Vivian on the side of her head.

She crashed to the floor.

Ben's arms around me never felt so good as I leaned against him. In spite of a tiny headache and being a tad dizzy, I felt wonderful.

"When I heard you shouting, I hung up and called Jerry right away." His breath tickled my ear. "To think you could have ended up like Honey."

"I didn't think Vivian would go berserk." We watched as an EMT checked Vivian, who'd been handcuffed and put on a stretcher. She probably had her own headache, judging by the goose egg on her noggin.

"This is all Honey's fault," Vivian muttered. "She could have left Curtis alone. But no. It was always about the money. Gabe Davis was a perfect suspect. Even Ben with those pictures. Or that Roland Thacker. Or Gretchen. Or Joe. Now I've lost everything. And I just don't care anymore."

Jerry turned after they wheeled her out the door to the ambulance outside. He turned to face me. "I'll get your statement. But first you need to go to the ER."

"I will."

Ben's arms tightened. What a wonderful man, and he was all mine. "I'll make sure she goes, Jer."

"Good. And we've got some news for you. Muscle Shoals PD called, and they picked up Curtis Delane trying to buy a bus ticket to LA. They're extraditing him back here for questioning. We should have enough to hold him for your aunt's death."

"Caught. Wow." How quickly circumstances changed. We weren't sure what would happen to the restaurant with Honey's sister challenging the will. Evidently visions of dollar signs danced in her head. But running a restaurant wasn't as easy as Gretchen probably thought it was. We decided to leave that part of our future in God's hands as we watched for new open doors.

"Thanks for letting us know." Ben kissed the top of my head.

The police left after taking some photos of the kitchen, and of me. Evidently my neck had started to bruise. When the house was quiet again, I heaved a sigh.

"I need to get that locket to momma. Vivian brought it and gave it to me today." I moved from Ben's arms and shivered as I approached the table. The golden heart felt warm to my hand. Its chain slid through my fingers.

Ben shook his head. "First things first. We've got to get your head checked. We need to make sure you don't have a concussion."

"Okay." The room tilted a bit. "That's a good idea."

"And then when the doctor says you're fine," he said as he took me in his arms again, "we need to see about starting that family."

My heart sang. "Ben, my love, that's a *very* good idea."

Lynette Sowell loves to spin adventures for the characters who emerge from story ideas in her head. She desires to take readers on an entertaining journey and hopes they catch a glimpse of God's truth along the way. Lynette is a Massachusetts transplant who lives in central Texas with her husband, two kids by love and marriage (what's a step-kid?), and five cats who have their humans well-trained. She loves to read, travel, spend time with her family, and also tries not to kill her houseplants, although her tropical hibiscus contemplated pressing charges after last winter. You can visit Lynette's Web site at www.lynettesowell.com

You may correspond with this author by writing:
Lynette Sowell
Author Relations
PO Box 721
Uhrichsville, OH 44683